WHEN KACEY LEFT

DAWN GREEN

Red Deer Press

Published in Canada by Red Deer Press, 195 Allstate Parkway, Markham,
Ontario L3R 4T8
Published in the United States by Red Deer Press, 311 Washington Street,
Brighton, Massachusetts 02135

www.reddeerpress.com

10 9 8 7 6 5 4 3 2 1

Red Deer Press acknowledges with thanks the Canada Council for the Arts,
and the Ontario Arts Council for their support of our publishing program. We
acknowledge the financial support of the Government of Canada through the
Canada Book Fund (CBF) for our publishing activities.

Canada Council   Conseil des Arts   ONTARIO ARTS COUNCIL
for the Arts   du Canada   CONSEIL DES ARTS DE L'ONTARIO
                                              an Ontario government agency
                                              un organisme du gouvernement de l'Ontario

Library and Archives Canada Cataloguing in Publication
Green, Dawn.
When kacey left / Dawn Green.
ISBN 978-0-88995-523-3
Data available on file.

Publisher Cataloging-in-Publication Data (U.S.)
Green, Dawn.
When kacey left / Dawn Green.
ISBN 978-0-88995-523-3
Data available on file.

Edited for the Press by Peter Carver
Cover and text design by Daniel Choi
Cover image courtesy of iStock
Printed in Canada by Friesens Corporation

MIX
Paper from
responsible sources
FSC® C016245
FSC
www.fsc.org

To everyone who has ever lost anyone

So like, the obnoxious counselor woman gave me this journal and is ~~asking telling~~ making me write these letters to you. She says it's a compromise—I say it's a punishment—because I don't like answering all her annoying questions.

"What would you like to talk about today?"—Nothing.

"How does that make you feel?"—I don't know.

"Let's explore that emotion..."—Let's not.

"Why do you think your parents have asked you to see me?"—Because they don't know what else to do with me.

"Would you like to talk about that?"—No. I don't want to talk. Not now. Not ever.

I have to start out each letter with "When you left ... something something something ..." It's supposed to help me deal with it or something. I think it's stupid. But she's watching me right now and, if I don't keep writing, she'll probably ask me more questions, so ... ugghhh ... fine, here I go ...

August 14ᵗʰ

Dear Kacey,

When you left, everything changed. I mean *everything*. You always hear adults saying some crap about how life can change in an instant. The kind of talk that always made you roll your eyes in that dramatic "please don't talk to me about this again" way. Don't talk to strangers. Don't stay out too late at night. Don't play with fireworks. Don't drink and drive—it's like, we know, already; leave it alone. But for real ... life really can change in an instant.

For me, the instant was that phone call from Drea. You know, she called me and asked if I'd heard the news, like it was the latest gossip and she had the first scoop or something. I could hear the excitement in her voice when I told her I hadn't heard anything about anything. Then she told me—

It was 11:14 in the morning—the "instant" when it all changed: 11:14. That time will never be the same for me again.

I was still sleeping. And when she told me, I actually thought I was still dreaming. Then my mom walked in and I saw the look on her face and I knew it was real.

Drea and I aren't friends anymore. Friends off!! Just one of the many life changes that happened after ...

To be honest, I think you were the only reason I was friends with her in the first place. Since you left, she's actually become kind of popular. I think everyone just feels bad for her. I think she's using the whole thing to get attention. The last thing I want is to talk to people about it. Which is why, I guess, everyone is so worried about me. My mom says that everyone deals with grief in a different way. Drea wants lots of friends around her and I don't want any. I just don't want anyone around me. Just leave me alone!!

I think that's all I want to write for now.

It's funny, the oc (obnoxious counselor) woman told me how to start but she didn't say how I should end.

Later, I guess.

Sticks

*August 17*th

Dear Kacey,

When you left, I had to start seeing this OC woman twice a week. It's summertime and there are so many places I'd rather be, things I'd rather be doing—okay, not true. I'd probably be in my room, staring at that stain on my ceiling that you said looks like an elephant. But still, it's summer and that's, like, sacred time. Granted, this is officially the crappiest summer ever but still, I should be allowed my own free time. Instead, I'm here, in this stupid yellow office that smells like vanilla candles (you know I hate vanilla). I obviously don't want to be here, but my mom says I have to go or I'm grounded. When she told me that, I slammed the door in her face and yelled, "Fine, then ground me." And I would have been totally fine with it, but then my dad came to talk with me and said that sometimes we have to do things we don't like so others can be happy ... or some crap like that. I don't really care if my mom's happy or not—I'm the one who lost a best friend—but then he told me that I'd get ten dollars every time I went (something I can't tell my mom).

So now I'm here and writing in this stupid journal because, every appointment, the OC checks to see that I'm writing something to you. She says she doesn't really read it, though, just kind of looks to see that I've written something. Not sure I believe her, but anyway, this is me, writing something.

This is so stupid.

Sticks

August 23rd

Dear Kacey,

When you left, I stopped sleeping. That's why it's 2:19 AM and I'm writing in this STUPID JOURNAL!! Not because I want to (let's be clear), only because I have nothing better to do.

I can't sleep. Well, I sleep sometimes—mostly in the day when I'm watching TV. It's just something about the night. I try falling asleep, but then I start thinking about you and I start to wonder where you are. Did you end up in heaven? You know how I feel about the whole church thing. I had to go, by the way, to your funeral. Well, they didn't call it a "funeral"; it was a "Celebration of Life"—like somehow that makes it all better. It didn't feel much like a celebration. It was awkward and weird. It felt like the whole school came out. Really, it was standing room only!!

Remember? We used to talk about stuff like that, wonder

who would come to our funerals if we died. Well, I can tell you that everyone came out for yours—all our friends, other students, kids we don't like, teachers from every grade, even our old French teacher Madam Girard, who we thought hated you, was there. I had to say hi and pretend to smile at so many people. My mom said it was the "right" thing to do. Everyone was talking about you. How they knew you. How they met you. When they met you. It all started to feel like one big game of who knew Kacey best. Like, who should be hurting the most or something.

I know it was your funeral but I hated it. Everywhere I went, someone was in my face. "Sara, I'm so sorry to hear about Kacey. How are you doing?"

"How the fuck do you think I'm doing?"—it's not what I said, but it's what I wanted to say. Although the F-word probably wouldn't have gone over too well in church.

"It's just sooooo sad ... soooo sad ... Soooo young"—that was said a lot.

Oh, and—"What a tragedy. Such a loss. Her poor family."

But the number one saying at your funeral has to have been: "It's just too bad. She's going to be missed." So there, people miss you already. I know I do. The whole time at the funeral, I kept thinking how I wish you were there so we could talk about it. But that would be weird, talking about your funeral at your funeral. Although, if you knew how many people were there or how many people were going to miss you, then maybe ... maybe things would be different.

Maybe we should all have living funerals so people can know how much they are loved. Maybe then they will know they're not alone.

Of course your family was there. Your mom was a mess and your dad stood at the back of the church the entire time. Owen sat next to me and didn't say anything. I think he was in shock or something. And don't worry, I'll keep an eye on him for you. Drea sat next to me, too. I think she liked that we got to sit at the front. She cried the entire time, and I'm not saying she wasn't sad but, after the first fifteen minutes, it felt really phony—like, enough already, we get it, you're sad. I'm just getting so annoyed with her.

You know what was really weird? Our entire Girl Guide group was there. My mom got mad because I kept looking back at them. She said that I needed to "pay attention," like we were in school or something. When did we stop going to Guides? Like, what, almost five years ago? But they were all there, dressed in blue and grouped together at the back of the church. You know those pictures of police and fireman funerals when all the officers are lined up in uniform to pay tribute? It was like that, but with pigtails and hand-sewn patches. I was waiting for them to give you some kind of a cookie salute. My mom says they were there because, again, it was the "right" thing to do. I didn't get it ... once a Guide always a Guide, I guess.

The church minister / reverend / priest guy spoke about the tragedy of losing someone so young and all that kind of stuff. He never said anything about heaven, though. I bet you're there, or somewhere nice. Sometimes I wonder if you're still here, like, in my room, right now, watching me write this. Are you? It would be so you to do that.

Just don't haunt me, okay?!!

Night.

Sticks

August 28th

Dear Kacey,

When you left, summer sucked. I honestly don't know why you left, but I *really* don't get why you had to leave during the summer. Why not before exams or January? Summer used to be our time. Don't you remember when we were little and we'd spend every night of the summer at each other's houses?! We used to get so excited about the summer that we'd start planning what we were going to do about a month before school ended.

There was that one summer when we planned to watch a hundred movies—we only made it to seventy-eight, but it was still an epic summer. Remember? We did it by making our own genres. I know you argued for B-movie horror week, but 80's teen classic week was / is still my favorite.

Then there was that other summer when we tried to

master a video game a week. Your mom got so mad at us for staying inside when it was nice out, but you came back with the best argument—"Mom, I know it's nice out, but we set a goal to master one game a week. You should be happy we're trying to achieve our goals." What's funny is that she left us alone after that. I think we ended up mastering seven games that summer.

And still, the title of "Best Summer Ever" has to go to the one when my parents took us on that camping road trip. We whined until they took us to every waterpark that we passed by. OMG, that was the road trip when you and I each had a vanilla milkshake from that sketchy-looking truck stop, and then we both got carsick. Well, technically, you got carsick first, and then the smell of it made me throw up as well. My parents were pissed, and then they made a rule that we couldn't drink any more milk products before a drive. We stayed up every night staring up at the stars, talking about everything and nothing, until we either fell asleep or my mom came out and made us go to bed.

You: See that star up there?

Me: I see a million stars.

You: That one. The one beside the big one that looks like it's blinking, almost.

Me: I think that's a satellite.

You: Shut up, it's a star.

Me: (laughing) Okay, whatever. What about it?

You: It's called Kaceyopia.

Me: It is not.

You: It is now. And that one, just below it, that's Saratarius. The legend is that ...

Me: What legend?

You: If you'd shut it, I'll tell you. Geez, interruptus, much?

Me: Sorry.

You: Okay, a long time ago, like a really long time, when there were Greek gods and monsters and stuff, there were these two best friends ...

Me: Let me guess, Kacey and Sara?

You: Princess Kacey and Princess Sara, to be exact. But they were from different kingdoms and their families were sworn enemies, so they had to keep their friendship a secret. One day Princess Kacey overheard the Queen plotting to destroy Princess Sara's family. She sent a ... a wizard named ...

Me: Zoltar

You: Really?

Me: Why not?

You: Okay, a wizard named Zoltar ... to cast a spell on the other kingdom. A spell that would put the entire kingdom to sleep forever. But Princess Kacey didn't want anything to happen to her friend, so she snuck out in the middle of the night, stole a horse, and fought countless monsters and dragons to reach Princess Sara before Zoltar could cast his spell.

Me: Wait. Doesn't Princess Sara get to fight monsters and dragons, too?

You: Uh, sure. They both fought monsters.

Me: And dragons.

You: Yes, and dragons. Anyway, fast forward: after Zoltar had put all of the kingdom to sleep, he stormed the castle where Princess Sara was waiting, and of course she bravely did everything she could to fight him off, but he was too powerful and, just as he was pointing his wand and casting his spell, Princess Kacey burst in and dove in front of Sara to save her.

Me: And what happened?

You: She was too late.

Me: What?!

You: It's not always a happily ever after. But, even though the spell hit both of them and they went to sleep forever, the power of their friendship turned them into stars, and now they are up there. And each time it looks like they are kind of blinking, it is actually the two of them laughing about their adventures together. The end.

Me: Kacey?

You: Ya?

Me: Why'd you leave?

You: You know I can't answer that. Look around; this is just a memory.

We didn't really plan out anything to do this summer. Actually, I don't think we were talking much in the spring.

This summer sucks.

Sticks

September 1st

Dear Kacey,

When you left ... Does this matter? You're gone and this letter-writing thing is bullshit ... blah, blah, blah. I HATE you, obnoxious counselor.

Fuck off.

Sticks

P.S. You know why it's bullshit? Because it's not going to bring you back—nothing is. When you left, you left. You're gone—GONE—and nothing I write in this journal is ever going to change that.

September 2nd

Dear Kacey,

When you left ... Why did you leave? I don't get it.
  Sticks

September 7th

Dear Stones, (I know you want me to write "Dear Kacey," you obnoxious counselor woman, but to me she was "Stones," so that's what I'm writing.)

When you left, life went on ... unfortunately. It's the first day of school and, even though I played the "dead friend" card and told my mom that I wasn't ready to see anyone yet, she made me go. The first day of every school year has always been awkward, but this year was especially awkward ... super awkward ... awkward of epic proportions.

Normally, I have you to hang with. Normally, we go together. This year, my dad drove me and, as soon as I stepped out of the car, I knew it was going to be a bad day. You know how movies always have that dream sequence, where someone dreams that they go to school naked and everyone is looking at them—pointing at them—whispering about them ... Well, I wasn't naked, but it felt a lot like I was the one in those dream sequences.

We had that first-day assembly in the theater and, when I walked in, I swear, everyone stopped talking and turned to look at me at the same time. Then there was a lot of whispering. All I wanted to do was scream, "YOU THINK I DON'T KNOW WHAT YOU'RE TALKING ABOUT?" But I didn't. I just stood there like an idiot, pretending like I didn't know everyone was staring at me while I looked for a place to sit.

I looked for Drea—I don't know why. Familiar face, I guess. She was sitting right in the middle of everyone, and I know she saw me. She looks different this year. She straightened her hair, and I'm pretty sure she's wearing more makeup. I heard that her parents gave her a lot of money after you left, to help her deal or something. She got money and I got therapy. Lame.

Anyway, as I was standing there looking like an idiot, I felt my phone vibrate. It was a text from Loren: *Come sit with me. Far left, second row.*

Me: Hey.
Loren: Hey.
Me: Thanks for saving me a seat.
Loren: Well, you looked kind of awkward standing at the front.
Me: Yeah, it felt like everyone stopped and looked at me when I walked in.
Loren: They did.
Me: Oh. I really hoped I was just imagining it.

Loren: You didn't. It was weird. But, whatever, it's their deal, not yours ... How you been?

Me: Okay. You?

Loren: You know ... hoping this year isn't going to totally suck.

Me: Me, too. Sorry I've been kind of ...

Loren: Nonexistent?

Me: Yeah.

Loren: I heard your parents made you go to a psychiatrist or something.

Me: Yep ... a counselor.

Loren: What's the difference?

Me: I don't know. I don't have to lie down on a couch or anything.

Loren: What do you do there?

Me: Talk. And she makes me write stuff down.

Loren: Like what?

Me: Just ... stuff. (I didn't want to tell her that I was writing to you.)

Loren: How's that going for you?

Me: It sucks.

Loren: It would. Did you get your course list?

Me: Yep. Here.

Loren: Cool. Looks like we've got English, Math, and Spanish together.

Me: Cool.

It was the first time that I'd talked to Loren since the funeral. She messaged me a few times on Facebook. I just didn't feel much like talking. I think she's a little pissed that I haven't talked to her in a while. It was nice of her to save me a seat, though.

The rest of the day was pretty uneventful—besides all the staring and whispering as I walked down the halls. I've kind of started getting used to it. I kind of have to.

Hasta luego.

Sticks

September 13th

Dear Stones,

When you left, things got weird. School is weird without you. Not weird in the way that everyone keeps pointing and whispering about me (because that's starting to feel normal), but weird in the way that I keep thinking I'm going to see you in the bathroom (where we used to meet all the time to just get away from class for a while), at my locker, in the lunchroom, pretty much everywhere. The worst is the hallway, because sometimes I actually think I do see you. Like today when I was going to the library, I thought I saw you walking down the hall away from me. For a moment I thought it was you. For a moment I forgot about everything and I almost called out your name. It was only for a moment, though, because then the girl turned around and she obviously wasn't you. She was some Grade 12 I've never seen before. But for that moment ... for just that one moment, it was you and everything was normal again.

Then another weird thing happened when I was in the library. And yes, if you're wondering, I've gone back to escaping into the library during breaks. I know you think it's where the "losers" hang out, but I like it there. It's quiet. It's away from everyone's stares and glares. It's a place where I can just ... be. So I don't care if you think that makes me a loser. Why was I telling you this? Oh, ya, the weird thing that happened ...

So there I was, minding my own business, tucked away in the corner of the history section, so I could read and secretly eat at the same time without the librarian kicking me out or telling me to throw away my lunch, when there was this girl watching me. I could feel her watching me before I saw her. You know that "creeper" feeling? So I looked up and saw her pretending to look at some books, when really she was looking at me. Watching me. I tried to just ignore her like I do everyone else, but this was different. She was different. I've never seen her before, so I think she must be in Grade 9. Her hair was in a ponytail and she was wearing a pair of those funky glasses that look like they're from the 50's—the ones with thick frames and pointy corners. You'd probably say they were cool and retro, but I don't think that's why she was wearing them. Anyway, she just kept watching me, even when she knew that I knew she was watching me. I tried to ignore her but, after ten minutes, I just couldn't anymore.

Me: What?

Weird Girl: (saying nothing)

Me: Can I help you?

Weird Girl: (still nothing)

Me (totally creeped-out at this point): WHAT'S YOUR PROBLEM?

Weird Girl: You're not supposed to yell in the library. And you're not allowed to eat in here, either.

And then she left. It was strange but, sadly, also the most exciting thing that happened today.

Sincerely,

Sticks (aka, the loser, who hides out in the history corner of the library)

September 18th

Dear Stones,

When you left, life got boring. There really is nothing to tell you right now but the OC is on me about writing you more. I don't know what to tell you. Things are fine. School is as boring as ever. I've been talking to Loren a bit more (mostly in class). Haven't talked to Drea at all.

My parents are back to their ignoring each other phase. For a while they were getting along again. Talking more, mostly about me and about you. They even started up date night again ... well, kind of. My dad wanted to take my mom out, but she told him she would rather stay home, order in, and rent a movie. It's because she doesn't want to leave me home alone at night. She told my dad that it was because she was tired, but he and I both know that she's scared to leave me alone. She's been like a 1950's TV mom ever since you left. She does my laundry, makes my bed, makes me breakfast every morning, prepares my lunch for me, is home when I get home, and asks me way too many questions about my day. It was nice for a while, but it's getting to be too much. I told her to back off the other day, that I just need some space away from her ... and then she started crying. Moms know how to make you feel guilty like no one else.

That's it. That's all that's been going on.

Sticks

September 21st

Dear Stones,

When you left, I became obsessed with you. Okay, I don't know if obsessed is what you'd call it—you probably would—but I have something to confess ... I've been watching you—a lot. Sometimes I spend hours in my room, just scrolling through my phone at old pictures and videos we took together. I can't stop. I've tried but it's like an addiction. My mom won't let me have my phone at dinner, and sometimes I just sit at the table, thinking about running back up to my room ... to be with you.

Photos of you. Of us. At the beach. At school. Your house. My house. Loren's house. Last Halloween. The movie theater. The mall—there's a ton of selfies we took in that hat store. Various parties ... there are even some I took at the party that night. You're not really in any of them, though, but if I zoom in, I can see you in the background. Like an eerie photobomb.

And I have that one video that I took of you singing at the beach. You're just sitting on a piece of driftwood, playing your guitar and coming up with random improvised lyrics. Then you turn your head and see that I'm holding up my phone. You ask me if I'm recording you and then you yell, drop the guitar, and come running after me. The video goes all crazy and it looks like an old episode from COPS, except that you can hear us both laughing hysterically. You wanted me to erase it ... I'm so glad I didn't.

I just keep watching it over and over and over again. I just want to hear your voice. I keep thinking I'm just going to listen to it one more time and then, as soon as it's over, I play it again.

I might have a problem.

Sticks

Sept 22nd

Dear Stones,

When you left ... you left—as in gone—not here—absent—
disappeared—missing—nonexistent ...

October 6ᵗʰ

Dear Stones,

It's been a while. You might not know that, because you're not actually here and I'm not actually writing you. This little realization is part of the reason why I haven't written in this thing for the last few weeks. When the OC asked me why I stopped writing to you, I kind of spazzed and told her it was stupid to write letters to someone who isn't here and can't read them ... or respond to them. My spazzout kind of worked because she said that I could take a break from the writing. I heard her tell my mom that I made some kind of breakthrough, and she thought the sessions were really helping me. BTW, I hate it when adults talk about you like you're not even there.

Anyway, according to the OC, the writing break is over and I have to start up again. Only this time I can do it my way,

none of the "when you left" stuff. I'm never going to tell the
OC or anyone else this, but I don't mind writing to you (for
the most part). To be honest, you're the only real friend I
have right now. How pathetic is that? My only real friend is
a dead friend who can't talk to me or write me back.

So, there are a few things I should update you on. Where
should I start?

Well, school still totally sucks. Nothing new there. Oh,
except that Weird Girl with the pointy glasses has become
my official stalker now. I see her everywhere. Or I should
say, she sees me everywhere. It's creepy. I'll be in the hall,
getting something out of my locker, and I can see her
watching me from the stairs. She's sitting on them and
pretending to read a book but, every time I glance over,
I can tell that she's looking at me, not the book. Or I'll be
coming out of a class and she'll just happen to be walking
by the door when I leave. I think she knows my schedule. I
know—I should be freaked out by this. And I'm not crazy—
Loren has seen her, too. We were standing in the cafeteria
line together and Loren was, like, "I think there's a girl over
in the corner staring at us." When I looked, for sure it was
her. I told Loren a little about the stalking stuff, which she
laughed hysterically at, and then I asked her if she knew
the girl and she said no, that she had never seen her before.
Here's the thing—the really strange thing: when I checked
her out in the yearbook, not only did I find her (her name's
Melissa Hunter), but she's in our grade and has been since
elementary school. How can I not recognize a girl that we
have gone to school with for years?

Are we all that invisible to one another?

I wonder if you knew her. Maybe a secret friend I didn't know about? Anyway, I finally tried to talk to her, and she just turned around and walked away. At least I know she's real and not some figment of my imagination. For a while, before Loren saw her, and before I looked her up in the yearbook, I was starting to think that I was going a little crazy. Like writing letters to my dead friend isn't enough!

Speaking of crazy—my mom and your mom have started to become friends. And by that I mean they talk on the phone and go for coffee and stuff. I know—crazy, right?! I didn't think they liked each other. Well, let's be honest, my mom didn't like your mom. But my mom doesn't really like anyone. Sometimes, I don't even think she likes me. No one can live up to her standards—that's something I heard my dad yell at her once. I didn't get it then but I do now. It's like we're not perfect enough for her. Nothing is ever good enough for her. Like she has this idea of what our lives should be like, and we're not living up to it. I think she still wants me to be the little girl who danced in pink tights and went shopping with her every Saturday. I can't help feeling that I'm not turning out the way she was hoping ... whoa ... off track ... Oh, the OC would love this. More crap about my messed-up life to talk about. If you're reading this, OC, just stop ... my mom and I have a great relationship and everything is just fine.

Anyway, back to our moms. I'm going to keep an eye on them. It's probably good for your mom that she has mine to talk to. I just hope my mom isn't doing this out of pity or something. I feel like your mom has been through enough lately.

Sticks

P.S. Seriously, OC, ignore what I wrote above about my mom. It's just normal teen / parent stuff. I'm fine. We're fine. I do NOT want to talk about it.

October 8th

Dear Stones,

I'm writing to you in English class. We have a new student teacher, Miss Baker. What a keener! We're about to start a poetry unit, and she's acting like it's the best thing ever. Ugh, I hate poetry. Why do they make us do this every year??

I remember you tried to get me to like it once. You told me to stop thinking about them like poems and start thinking about them like song lyrics. You said—and I quote—"Everything is better if it is set to music." You thought music could fix anything ... but I guess it couldn't fix everything.

So I moved to the back of the class. It's better here. No one can look at me without me knowing. Even though the new teacher is super peppy and hyper all the time, I kind of like her. She doesn't look at me the way everyone else does. I guess she doesn't know. Drea is in this class, too, and—

surprise, surprise—she is sitting in the middle. Center stage, right where she wants to be. Loren sits in the back with me—not next to me, though; she's across the room. All she ever does is draw in her notebook and stare at Mateo.

I like it back here. I've got the corner by the window and Jake, that big hockey kid who is almost never here, sits next to me. If he ever comes to class, he's usually sleeping. Apparently he's headed for the NHL or something. Don't you have to pass school to play in the NHL? OH, GOD, now Baker is reading out a poem in front of the class. She's actually standing on the desk and trying to say it like a rapper—a small white-girl rapper. Everyone's laughing at her and taking pictures with their cell phones. You'd be rolling your eyes and making so much fun of her right now ... actually, I think you'd like her, too. The bell just went.

Later.

Sticks

P.S. Two sightings of Weird Girl today.

October 10*th*

Dear Stones,

Señor Fuckhead confiscated my phone in Spanish class today. It's not like I was bothering anyone, or like we were doing anything that mattered. He was up at the board, going over the past tense—which I aced on the last quiz, BTW—and then he just came over and took it out of my hand. He said some bullshit about not paying attention in class and then put it in his desk. The whole class "ooohed" like it was some big deal. Asshole.

When I went to get it from him after class, he told me that next time I tried to text during his class, he would send it and me to the office. I told him that I wasn't texting, I was looking at pictures of you. I wasn't trying to play the sympathy card (not really); it was the truth, but it worked like a charm, because he got really awkward and looked like he felt really bad. He actually apologized and told me that if I ever felt like I needed some time to myself, to just tell him and he'd let me go to the bathroom, or whatever. I'm still pissed that he took my phone in the first place, but I guess he's a nice guy. I'm just glad he didn't tell my parents— that's all I need right now.

Sticks

October 12th

Stones,

I've been thinking about death a lot. And I've been thinking about you. Wondering how it felt, if it hurt, if you were scared, if you thought about me ... and then I think about how selfish I'm being, wondering if your last thoughts were about me. I do wonder about your last thoughts a lot, though. I've been thinking a lot about death since the whole thing happened. I'm not telling anyone about that, though. It would just freak them out. They're already freaking out enough.

I've got people watching me all the time. My mom is always poking her head in and wondering how I'm doing. That OC won't leave me alone. The teachers at school keep looking at me during class. Then I catch them looking, and they get all uncomfortable and pretend they were doing something else. I think they're scared I'm going to do something crazy. All I feel like doing is taking off for a while. All I want is to be alone for a little while, maybe go to that place on the beach where you and I used to go when we wanted "Sticks and Stones" time. I'm not sure if I'll ever be alone again. I feel like I'm in a prison, surrounded by a cage of people who won't let me out of their sight. I get it, though. I think they all think that they're doing the right thing. Maybe if I hadn't left you alone ... probably wouldn't have changed anything. Right?

Sticks

October 14th

Dear Stones,

You know "The Famous Published Wall of Work in English?"
The one with stuff up there from all the way back to the
60's? The one that Mr. Harper made a ginormous deal
about when a student wrote something that according to
him was "so amazing ... so fantastic ... so brilliant ..." it
deserved to be published and added to the wall. The one
that he told us stays up FOREVER so future generations
will have something to aspire to. That wall!! Well, I guess
forever doesn't include you anymore because, I'm sorry to
break it to you, there's an empty space where your poem
(I think it was a poem—about the ocean? Or was it rain?)
used to be. And it is so obvious that something is missing,
because now there's just this dark blue rectangular shape
with a paler-blue sun-faded border around it—bordering

nothing. And I can't stop looking at it.

What do they think? We won't think about you if we can't see any of your things around? That they can just slowly disappear pieces of you and we won't notice? Won't remember? It's like some sci-fi dystopian novel where the government tries to manipulate the past, thinking that the citizens just won't notice. Next they're going to try and remove that section of my memory ... although, sometimes I wonder if that would be so bad. It probably wouldn't hurt as much as this.

They also moved your desk to the side where all the dictionaries are stacked. I know it was your desk because, from where I'm sitting, I can still see where you carved: *K-STONZ sits here.* Do they think the desk is cursed or something? The "death" desk!? It's just a desk, people. Don't know why I'm telling you this. Just thought you should know.

Oh, and I took a piece of paper and wrote: KACEY'S (AKA, STONES) POEM WAS HERE, and put it up on the published board when no one was around. I thought you should know that, too.

Sticks

P.S. Only one sighting of Weird Girl today.

October 15th

Dear Stones,

I haven't cried yet. I think that's what everyone is waiting for. It's not like I haven't tried to cry. I spend hours in the bath trying to cry. I even bring my phone in and scroll through pictures of us sometimes.

I keep staring at that one of you and me in the food court at the mall. It's the one where you've got a straw up your nose. There's banana-chocolate milkshake slowly dripping out the end of it, and I'm pointing at you, laughing hysterically.

Then there's the one at my sixteenth birthday. I wanted to have everyone over for a giant sleepover, but my mom made those reservations at that fancy restaurant on the water and rented us that limo. It wasn't what I wanted but, I have to admit (although I'll never tell my mom), the limo was fun. Remember? We looked for nice dresses to wear for, like, weeks? You couldn't decide on anything, and then finally we found you the perfect one on that discount rack. It was blood red, and you said it would look good with black hair, which you didn't have at the time, so we bought hair dye and came back to the house. You wanted me to dye my hair with you but I couldn't. You were always so much braver than I was. Your parents were so mad, but you know what? You looked good, and you were right—I'm looking at the pic right now—the red does look good with black hair.

I'm going to do it, K ...

... Well, I dyed my hair black. My mom is freaking out right now. I'm up in my room, and I can still hear her yelling at my dad about the whole thing. He's telling her that it's just a phase, but she's afraid that I'm ... she's just worried about me. They've been arguing a lot lately. It's usually about me. Whether or not I should go to school. Whether or not I should be seeing that obnoxious counselor. Whether or not I should eat dinner. Whether or not I'm spending too much time in my room.

Yesterday, my mom told me to put on a jacket, and I told her I didn't want to, and then they started to argue about that. I knew that I needed a jacket—it was freezing outside—but when my mom told me to put one on, I snapped, "NO," without really thinking about it. I still don't know why. She just ...

ARGHHHH!! ... You know??!! I really wish she'd just leave me alone. This is why I hate being an only child. Anyway, I dyed my hair. I think it looks good and, like you told me, it really makes my green eyes pop.

I think you'd like it.

Sticks (with black hair)

October 18th

Dear Stones,

So the whole hair-dyeing thing has become ... a thing. People are kind of going crazy because of it. Seriously, who would have thought that me dyeing my hair would cause this many problems? First, it was my mom, then the OC was all worried about why I decided to do it—I think my mom was talking to her. And then Drea cornered me in the school bathroom. At first, she didn't say anything. I was washing my hands when she came in to fix her hair or makeup or something. She looked at me, made some kind of snarky huff sound, and then took out her lip-gloss. When I asked her what her problem was, she said that everyone was talking behind my back about how I was trying to turn into you, and then she said my hair looks just as stupid on me as it did on you ... anyway, we got into a fight.

The whole school is saying that I punched her, but that didn't happen. It was more of a yelling match, and I grabbed her purse and threw all her makeup in the toilet. That new student teacher, Miss Baker, heard us and came in. We both had to go to the office, but they let Drea go and I had to talk with Mr. Kline—of course.

Here's how that went ...

Kline: Sara ... How are you doing?

Me: (shrugging) Fine, I guess.

Kline: Is it true that you dumped Ms. Sheppard's belongings into the toilet?

Me: Yes, but she ...

Kline: Look, Sara, we all know that you are dealing with something very difficult. However, that doesn't give you the right to destroy another person's property or act out in this manner.

Me: I didn't destroy it. It just got a little wet.

Kline: Miss Stickley, what you did is serious. I hope you're not amused by this.

Me: No, sir. (I admit, I might have said it with a little sarcasm.)

Kline: You're putting me in a difficult position here. I understand that you miss your friend. What happened to Kacey was a tragedy. But you need to understand that there are others dealing with the same loss, and each of you is going to deal with it in your own way. You need to respect that some ...

Me: Why hasn't the school done anything?

Kline: What do you mean?

Me: A service, an assembly, something? And why are you taking down all her stuff? What did you do with her poem? It's like you're all just trying to sweep her away.

Kline: I'm sorry you feel that way. As you know, we have counselors available to any student who feels they need to talk with someone and help them to understand or deal with this difficult time. We are just trying to do what we think is best. Please know that an assembly was discussed by the administration, but it was thought best to keep things simple and not glorify what happened.

Me: Glorify?

Kline: Perhaps glorify is not the best word. What I meant to say was that we don't want students thinking that something like this will gain them attention.

Me: What are you saying? You think everyone will start doing what Kacey did so they can be popular or something? That's stupid.

Kline: No ... I think you're misunderstanding me ...

Me: I don't. I think I totally get it.

Kline: Sara, this is a complicated matter. We understand that a lot of students and faculty are upset by what happened, and that's why we are trying to get through this with as little change as possible. Keep things normal.

Me: (mumbling) Normal? Whatever.

Kline: In saying this, I noticed that you have dyed your hair.

Me: So? It's my hair.

Kline: Absolutely, it is your hair ... however, the color

you chose might be offensive to some of those who are mourning the loss of Miss Anders.

Me: Offensive?

Kline: Distasteful—again, we need to be respectful of those around us.

Then he told me it would be a good idea to dye my hair back to normal, and you know what I said? "Fuck that." I actually said that ... to the principal!! I know. It just came out before I could stop myself. You should have seen the look on his face. Apparently, the whole school is talking about that, too. I have no idea how they know that happened. I apologized right away. But he suspended me anyway. It's not a real suspension. It won't go on my record or anything. He said I should just "take some time." Time for what, I don't know, but it lets me miss some school, so, whatever. And he gave me your poem. Said I could keep it. It was in a file. Your file. The "Kacey" file—which was actually pretty thick. I couldn't see everything, but it looked like it was mostly full of your work ... pieces of you.

Oh, and BTW, to top things off, on my way out of the office, I saw Weird Girl. She was in that room near the office where kids with special needs and learning disabilities go. Maybe that's why no one has ever seen her before. Maybe she's "special." And if she is, I just feel bad for thinking she's weird. Maybe she can't help it. From now on, I'll refer to her as "Glasses Girl."

Anyway, back to what happened in the office. I can't believe some of the things that Dictator Kline said. They don't want to "glorify" what happened. And he tried to take it back but I know that's what he meant. And "keep things normal"—really? Like any of this is "normal."

How can things ever be normal again?

And, as if my hair has anything to do with anything. It's like they all think if we just don't talk about it, then it will go away. I've tried that. Doesn't work. Not that I want to talk about it all the time (OC, if you're reading this, I don't want to talk about it). I just mean we can't ignore what happened to you. It still happened. And it still hurts, whether I try to ignore it or not.

So now, with me home and suspended, Dictator Kline can relax a little. He'd probably kick me right out of the school if he could. Get rid of the problem.

Being suspended doesn't totally suck, except that I'm not allowed on the Internet. Also, my mom is too scared to leave me at home alone, so she and my dad have each taken turns to stay home from work. Today is Dad's day. Thankfully, he's downstairs watching some sport highlights or something. He calls up every now and then to ask if I want something to eat, but that's about it. The truth is, we haven't really talked since ... since it happened. He's never been much of a talker.

I really wish you were here for all this.

Sticks

P.S. I don't care what my mom or Dictator Kline or anyone else thinks. I'm keeping the hair.

October 19th

Dear Stones,

Day two of my suspension. Today my mom is home with me. We've already fought three times and it's only 10:34 AM ... this is going to be the longest day ever!!

The first time was over me not eating breakfast. I'm not hungry; leave me alone.

The second time was about why I threw Drea's makeup in the toilet. She's a bitch and she deserved it; leave me alone.

The third time was because I locked the door to my room and wouldn't let her in. I want to be alone, SO LEAVE ME THE FUCK ALONE!

Anyway, as I write this, I am sitting on the couch in the TV room, pretending to do homework while my mom watches some talk show about loser makeovers. Every now and then, she glances over to make sure I'm not doing "anything." The truth is, I can't do any homework because I already did it yesterday. How lame am I? So lame I've done all my homework and even read ahead in all of my classes. My best friend just died. It's like the best excuse in the world to not do my homework and not care about school, and here I am getting ahead of everyone else. All the grief books in the obnoxious counselor's office say that it's normal for grades to start slipping, but mine have actually gone up. I'm like the worst grieving friend ever. I'm getting good grades and I still haven't cried.

I just got a text from Loren. She says that everyone is talking about me at school. The new rumor is that I was cutting myself in the bathroom when Drea walked in. Apparently, I threatened her with a knife. I bet Drea started that. She's such a Drama Queen. I don't know why everyone is so worried that I'm going to start hurting myself just because you're gone. That's a bit drastic, don't you think? They all think I've gone crazy but, really, they need to look in the mirror. Take my mom, for example—every thirty seconds she looks over at me to make sure I'm still here and not doing anything weird ... she just looked ... again ... again ... again ... I mean, is this normal behavior?

Hahahahaha ... I just got sent to my room for giving my mom the finger. I couldn't help myself. You should have seen the double-take when she looked over at me.

Classic!

Sticks

Rain

Vapor formation
Cloud creation

Birthed of a storm
Life takes form

Ethereal particles plunging
Covert paratroopers with unknown orders

Crashing
Splashing
Causing uncontrollable ripples

Sinuous stream
Sinuous connections
Swept away in the flow
Swept away by the pull

Current takes hold
The battle-weary weaken
Just let go

Assimilation
Acculturation

Survival by any other name
would taste as bitter

Estuary respite
Ocean invite

Drop

~ By Kacey Anders

You: What are you doing?
Me: Reading your poem. Did you really have to use such big words?
You: I like words. I like how they sound and how they roll

off the tongue, like sinuous, and how they can feel almost
as if you're chewing them, like acculturation.

Me: I don't know. It seems pretty ...

You: Pretentious?

Me: Snobby.

You: They're just words, Sticks.

Me: Are they?

You: What do you think you'll find?

Me: Nothing. I don't know.

You: I'm not in there.

Me: I know.

You: What you're looking for isn't in there, either.

Me: How do you know I'm looking for something?

You: Because I know you.

Me: But did I know you?

Dear Stones,

It's still October 19th and still day two of my suspension. I'm
up in my room, and I've been reading and re-reading your
poem for hours. I had to look up what some words meant.
Ethereal? Sinuous? Acculturation? Really??!! Who uses
those words?!

I think I understand why they took it down.

One of the many things I hate about English class is the
way they make us analyze everything over and over again,
looking for hidden symbolic meanings and dissecting every
little word, until all that's left is nothing more than ink in the
shape of letters on paper. That's where you and I were so
different. You loved all that arty English shit.

Before ... I wouldn't have seen anything. Just fancy big words on paper.

But now, after ... I see things. I mean, I think I see things. Things that I should have seen before. Things that make more sense now. But maybe it's also nothing. Just words on paper that I want to mean something—and this is why I hate English!!!!

Is this you?

uncontrollable ripples ... crashing ... assimilation ... just let go ...

Just. Let. Go.

Are these just words?

Sticks

October 20th

Dear Stones,

Apparently, I've gone crazy and threatened everyone in school ... at least that's what the new rumor is.

So here's what's going on. It's day three of suspension and, today, they got my grandma to come and babysit. She's cool, though. She tried to talk to me about you a little bit. She asked a few questions about how I was doing, told me some stories about how she's lost a lot of friends, which was totally depressing, and then she left to go and make cookies. She says that she misses you, by the way.

Why does everyone want me to talk about you? You were my best friend and you're gone now. I'm dealing.

Anyway, the really cool thing is that she's letting me use the computer. I guess Mom and Dad forgot to tell her that I was grounded from the Internet. I went on FB and saw that people are trying to find out what happened at school. Drea's page is covered with questions and concerns. Her # of friends just hit 400. From 98 to 400 in a couple of weeks— that has to be some kind of record.

I think the thing that's bothering me the most is that she's acting like SHE was your best friend. I mean, really? You two met in Grade 8. You and I have been friends since the first day of Grade 3. I know you would say that it's not a competition, but it's bothering me that she's acting like she's lost her best friend in the whole world when, really, it's me.

I did have one friend request, though, and it's so weird. It's Jake Landry, that hockey guy who sits next to me in English class. We've never spoken to each other, and now he wants to be my FB friend?? What's up with that? I accepted, so I guess we'll see. Loren also wrote me a message. She wants to know if we can hang out this weekend, so I told her to come over for a sleepover on Saturday. We see each other at school and stuff, but we haven't really done anything together since ... that night. We're not really "friends on" or "friends off" ... we're just kind of "friends paused," I guess.

I also checked your page. It's still there. It'll probably be there forever. Your profile pic is the one I took of you two summers ago. We must have spent our entire vacation hanging out on that beach. You're swinging off that Arbutus tree with the ocean in the background, making that stupid monkey face that always made me laugh. Hundreds of people wrote on your page. It's all good things. How much they miss you; what a nice person you were; how cool you were; how sorry they are; they hope you're in a better place, etc. ... Your last post was a quote from Dr. Seuss: *Today was good. Today was fun. Tomorrow is another one.* You wrote that two days before ...

I think it's weird that you're gone but your FB page is still here. And I guess it's going to stay like that forever. Is that what is going to happen to all of us? We'll all be long gone, but fragments of us (emails, blogs, texts, tweets, pictures, FB) will remain online like an immortal cyber-existence. And what if it all crashes? Then what will be left of us?

So that's been my day. I'd ask how yours has been but you're not here—you're not here.

Sticks

Can't believe I'm going to say this, but I'm actually missing school. Being home is giving me too much time to think. And think about you. And thinking about you makes me miss you more.

WHY??

Why the fuck would you do that to yourself?

You're an idiot.

I really didn't mean that.

No, actually, I kind of did.

October 24th

Dear Stones,

I don't know what to say.

I stopped writing to you for a couple of days. I even threw this notebook in the garbage on Friday, but then Miss Baker found it, and I had to stay after school and talk with her ... SO AWKWARD!

Baker: How are you doing?
Me: Good.
Baker: Really?
Me: Yep.
Awkward silence
Me: I'm sorry about the other day ... what happened in the bathroom.
Baker: That's okay. It's the first time I've ever had to deal

with a disciplinary issue.

Me: (laughing a little) Well, it's the first time I've ever been a disciplinary issue.

Baker: I'm sorry you got suspended. I think they were a little harsh with you.

Me: (shrugging) I probably deserved it. I did swear at Mr. Kline.

Baker: Yeah, that might not have been the best idea. Sara, I think I should tell you that I know about what you've been going through.

Me: (nothing)

Baker: I'm sorry that you're dealing with so much right now. I found this notebook in the trash. I think it belongs to you.

Me: Uh, thanks.

Baker: I only read enough to know that it was yours.

Me: Okay.

Baker: I think it's really great that you're doing that. Writing things down can really help ... sort things out. It helps us muddle through all those thoughts and emotions we don't know what to do with.

Me: You sound like my ob ... counselor.

Baker: Is that a good thing or bad?

Me: (shrugging)

Baker: I hope you're not thinking of stopping. I don't think you've said everything you need to say to her.

Me: I thought you didn't read it.

Baker: I didn't. I just think that if you're throwing it in the garbage, then you're probably not done with it.

There were a few more awkward pauses, but that was pretty much it. She's kind of cool, I guess ... for a teacher.

School that day totally sucked. No one talked to me. Of course, I didn't really want them to, anyway. I think I'm becoming the odd kid that everyone avoids.

Remember Evan J. in the fourth grade? He always smelled like sour milk and sat by himself on the tire chair in the playground, reading the same stained Archie comic over and over again. I think I'm getting to be like him, minus the sour milk smell and Archie comic. I wonder whatever happened to that kid. Didn't he go to some "special" school after Grade 6? Maybe they'll send me to a "special" school soon.

I'm sorry I got so mad at you the other day.

Sticks

P.S. Even Glasses Girl is avoiding me. I didn't see her at all today. Is it strange that I kind of miss her?

October 25th

Dear Stones,

Loren and I have officially stopped hanging out. She was going to come over for a sleepover tonight but I bailed on her. I made my mom phone and tell her mom that I wasn't feeling well. I don't know why, I just don't want to talk to her about ... well, about you. And I know that's what she wants to do.

I just found out that her parents made her go to a counselor as well. She didn't tell me herself, though. I only know because her mom told my mom and my mom told me, to make me feel better about going. Yay, I'm not the only freak around. My mom totally doesn't get it. She's mad that I canceled on Loren but I don't care. I can hear her and my dad fighting about it downstairs.

Mom: Why do you keep defending her? She needs to spend time with some real friends.

Dad: Just leave her be. If she doesn't feel up to it ...

Mom: Oh, she's feeling fine. She just wants to hide up in her room, listening to music all night. It's not healthy. She needs real friends.

Dad: Give her time.

Mom: She's had enough time.

Dad: Has she? I know I never had to deal with what she's going through at her age.

Mom: I know. You're right. I'm just ... worried about her.

I can't believe my dad won that one. He never wins.

My mom's wrong. I'm not up here listening to music. I'm not up here doing anything other than writing to you. I kind of stopped listening to music. No, I'm serious!! I haven't touched my iPod in forever. I don't even know where it is— probably under a pile of clothes or something.

There's this song playing on the radio right now. I don't know who it's by, but the lyrics are something about coming home and washing away pain and sins ... I fucking HATE this song right now. People are posting it on your FB, dedicating it to you and shit like that. Some are sending it to me because it reminds them of you. What's funny is that I know you'd hate this song. We would have made so much fun of it together. But it's EVERYWHERE!! It's hard to listen to anything right now. Everything reminds me of you. Reminds me of something we did together. Like that Damien Rice song we listened to on repeat. And I know you don't agree with me, but you got so good at playing it on the guitar. Every time I listen to the part at the end, the part where it gets fast, it always makes me think about how frustrated you got when you messed up, and then how mad you got when I laughed at you for getting frustrated ... I hate music.

    You: You don't mean that.
    Me: Yes, I do.
    You: Sticks.
    Me: Okay, I don't hate it ... it's just that it doesn't sound the same without you. And when I listen to it ... I just ... I see you. It's like a montage of you running through my head.
    You: A montage of me? Like my greatest hits?
    Me: Kind of.
    You: I like that.
    Me: You would.
    You: You have to listen to music, Sticks. You have to listen to it for me because I couldn't take it if I wrecked music for you.
    Me: It doesn't sound the same without you. Nothing's the same without you.
    You: Is that why you bailed on Loren?
    Me: Hanging out with her reminds me too much of hanging out with you. All of us together. And I can't do it. It hurts too much.

You're gone but you're not really gone. And it hurts.
Sticks

October 27th

Dear Stones,

You never told me you were leaving. The OC asked me what your last words were to me. I told her I didn't remember, because it's none of her freaking business, and because it's a lot more fun to be difficult with her.

You said, "See ya later." Those were your exact words. "See ya later." See-ya-later, and then you left me at that party on the beach. What if I'd left with you? If you came over to my house for a sleepover that night instead? If only I told you that I wanted you to stay with me that night. But I stayed with Loren, and you ... you left.

See ya later.

Sticks

October 29th

Dear Stones,

It's official—I've become the weird kid at school. I think I'm even weirder than Glasses Girl.

Everyone's still avoiding me. I sit at the back of the class; I go to the library and read during breaks; and at lunch I wait till almost everyone has left the cafeteria before I go in, or I just avoid lunch altogether. I think it's why I've lost some weight. My mom is super worried I have some kind of eating disorder now. She sends me to school with lunch and, most days, I try to eat what I can, but sometimes I don't get to it and I forget to dump it out (like today), and she freaks out. I admit that I should be eating more. It's not like I'm doing it on purpose. And it's not like I'm not eating at all. She watches me eat dinner right in front of her, and I snack as soon as I get home. Sometimes I'm just not hungry. But sometimes I do just want to avoid the lunchroom.

I hate the lunchroom. I've always hated the lunchroom, but I hate it even more now. It's supposed to be a place where the school comes together but, really, it just separates us more. You know what it's like? It's like a giant ring of popularity. Or like a giant circus ring. There are the freaks and social outcasts (like me) who eat on the outskirts of the room. The next ring in is the geeks/nerds, Asian kids, and foreign exchange students. Kind of mixed in that group are the pot-heads who sit with their head phones on all day. Then there are the drama kids, artsy students, club groups, and those that aren't trying to be cool but kind of are, because they're not trying (I think we used to sit with them). And then the jocks and team sport people, and next to them, right in the middle, there's the popular crowd— the ringleaders (or the ones that think they are). Drea is sitting in that center circle now—sitting in the middle of the ring. Like a bull's-eye. It's where she's always wanted to be. Loren's kind of a floater, but she usually sits in the artsy group circle with Mateo, and Jake sits with the jocks. I don't know where Glasses Girl sits. She's never in here. I don't know why I'm finding this so fascinating.

And here's me, on the outside.

Sticks

*October 30*th

Dear Stones,

So I came home from school today and my dad was sitting in the living room, waiting for me. He said he had a surprise for me, and then took me into the kitchen, and there was this cardboard box on the floor. You're not going to believe this, but he got me a dog—a puppy, actually.

>   *Me*: What's this?
>   *Dad*: A puppy!
>   *Me*: I can see that, Dad.
>   *Dad*: (with a stupid silly smile on his face) Isn't she cute?
>   *Me*: She?
>   *Dad*: Yeah, the breeder only had one female left, and I thought she'd be perfect for you.
>   *Me*: For me?

Dad: Don't you like her?

I did think she was really cute. Who doesn't think a puppy is cute?! But for some reason, I couldn't say that to him. I know he wanted me to jump up and down and get really excited about the whole thing, but all I felt was anger.

Me: What kind is she?
Dad: A chocolate Lab. You don't sound excited. You're not happy I got her for you? You've been asking for a dog since you were six.
Me: Ya, when I was six, I wanted a dog. You and mom both said we couldn't get one and you got me a hamster instead.
Dad: Well, I think maybe now the time is right.
Me: The time? You mean this time, right now, after my best friend died? NOW YOU DECIDE TO GET ME A DOG?
Dad: Sara, calm down. She isn't supposed to be some replacement for ...
Me: Oh, really?!
Dad: Really. I just thought ...
Me: Does Mom even know?
Dad: Not yet.
Me: She's going to lose it.
Dad: You let me handle her. I'm not trying to replace Kacey with her—I just thought that you could, you know, use a friend.
Me: Because I don't have others?
Dad: That's not what I meant. Look, do you want me to take her back?

Of course I told him no. She's freaking adorable. She's this soft fluffy chocolate ball with bright green eyes. Only Cruella de Vil would send her back.

I brought her up to my room and, right now, she's jumping around my floor, playing with a ball of socks.

I am excited he got her for me, but I'm also pissed off because I KNOW the only reason he did it was because of you.

Oh, Sara, your best friend died. That's too bad. Here's a dog.

I'm not two. They can't just distract me and make everything all better by buying me something.

I made my dad feel bad. I get that he's trying to do something for me, it's just ... I don't know ... when I look at her, all I can think is that she's here and you're not. And if you were here, he never would have gotten her for me. It's so fucked up.

And now I can hear my parents fighting downstairs. My mom is pissed that he didn't tell her about it. She just said that she wants him to return it, and he yelled back, "NO! You can deal with Sara your way, and I can deal with her mine!" Deal with me. See, I told you this was about you.

My parents have been fighting a lot lately. After your funeral, things were better with them but, lately, it's gone back to normal, to before you left—actually, I think they're more divided than before. My dad's been sleeping in the spare room, although he keeps making the bed before I get up and pretending that everything's fine. I only know because I'm still not sleeping and, every now and then, when I get up for some milk, I can hear him snoring. They're acting like I'm the one who left, or I did something to them, or like you left them and not me.

And now there's this dog. I don't even know what to call her. Oh, friggin' fantastic, she just peed on the floor. My mom's going to throw a conniption if I don't clean it up.

Sticks

~~October 31st~~ *November 1st*

Dear Stones,

I have a lot to tell you. Something BIG happened with Weird Glasses Girl (and I've gone back to calling her Weird because, well ... you'll understand when I tell you what happened). But I'll get to that.

So, my mom made me go to the Halloween Dance because she thinks I'm staying in my room too much. I would have ditched but, not only did she make me go, she signed up to help with the refreshments table to make sure that I went! As if going to the dance wasn't bad enough. And I had to dress up. The only thing we had around the house was that old witch's costume I wore in Grade 7. Original, I know. Oh, and the best part—my mom went as a witch, too. She was so excited that we were matching. She even made my dad take a picture before we left. I know it sounds lame, and it was, but my mom was so happy that I was getting out of the house and that we were matching ... the smile on her face, I just couldn't take that away. Besides, it was just one night and, let's be honest, it's not like it was going to hurt my popularity. I've definitely invented a new low on the popularity food chain.

The Halloween Dance—I don't know why they call it a dance. No one is there to actually dance. There's music, and they had one of those big screens with videos playing on it, but everyone was just standing around and talking. Honestly, it was the longest two hours of my life. It wasn't a dance; it was torture. And, yes, it was *that* bad. I talked with Loren for a bit, but she was there to see Mateo, so we didn't hang out for long. Drea and her group of wannabes came dressed in next to nothing. Really, I think they only like Halloween because they can get away with wearing things that they couldn't during school. Sometimes I can't believe Drea. If things were normal ... if you weren't gone and we were all still friends, she would have been making fun of those girls with us. I don't know what she's doing with them. Whatever.

My mom wanted me to stay close, but I kept getting "the look" from everyone who saw me there so, as soon as she was busy, I snuck out and went for a walk around the hallways.

I saw Jake with some of his hockey buddies by the back door, taking swigs from a water bottle. They think they're so sneaky, but it doesn't take a brainiac to know it's not water in the bottle ... idiots. Some of them saw me when I walked by. I could hear them whispering and laughing about me. I'm not sure, because I left too quickly, but I think I saw Jake hit one of the guys who said something about me. I'm pretty sure he did. I didn't want to go back to the dance, so I kept walking around.

A school is an eerie place at night when no one is around. I went by your locker. They took down all the notes and flowers people had taped to it. No one is using it yet. I don't think anyone wants to. It just felt so empty. I don't know why I did it, but I got a jiffy marker from my locker and wrote on the inside of yours: *K-stonz was here*.

It was permanent marker, so I don't think they'll be able to erase it. I hope they don't.

Then things got "weird." I was walking back to the dance when I saw Weird Glasses Girl standing at the end of the hallway looking at me.

Let me set the scene.

The hall was dark. There was no one else around. I was standing at one end of the hall and she was standing at the other, staring at me. Oh, and she was dressed as a clown, and you know how clowns freak me out! The only reason I knew it was her was because of her glasses. It felt like something right out of a horror movie. She started walking toward me. Came right up to me. I wanted to run but I stood my ground ... and that's when she started talking to me.

Weird Girl: What are you doing?
Me: Nothing.

WG: Yes, you were. I saw you putting graffiti on the lockers.

Me: What?

WG: I saw you.

Me: So what? It's my friend's locker.

WG: Was.

Me: WHAT?

WG: She's not here anymore.

Me: What do you want? Why are you always following me?

WG: How did she do it?

Me: As if I'd tell you.

WG: But you know, don't you?

Me: You're a freak.

WG: My dad says that it's not nice to call people names.

Me: Get out of here. Leave me alone.

WG: He also says that she didn't go to heaven.

Me: WHAT?!

WG: And he's a minister, so he would know.

Me: Is that why you've been following me like a freak?

WG: He said people like her are lost and always will be.

Me: You shut the fuck up. You didn't know her.

WG: You shouldn't swear. My dad says that she ...

Me: SHUT UP. Shut the FUCK up ...

And that's when Miss Baker walked in—dressed as an angel!! She had heard me yelling from down the hall and came to see what was going on. It's a good thing, too, because I was going to hit Weird Girl. I've never hit anyone before—okay, maybe you, during a pillow fight or something, but this was different. I wanted to hit her, punch her, push her, something. She took off as soon as Baker arrived. All she saw was me standing alone in the hall. I was so mad that I was shaking, actually shaking. I didn't even know that was a real thing.

Baker: Sara, are you all right? What happened?

Me: That's not true.

Baker: What's not true?

Me: That she's not in heaven. That's not true. It's not true. It's not. Why would she say that?

Baker: Maybe we should go back to the dance. Find your mom.

Me: I don't want to go back there. Why would she say that? Why?

Baker: Well ... some people believe ...

I didn't wait to hear the rest of what she was going to say. I couldn't. I just took off and ran all the way home and started writing.

All this time. All this time, wondering why Weird Girl was following me ... and THAT's why? I hate her. FREAK!

I know it's not true. Your family isn't even religious. It can't count if you don't believe in it. Right?

It's 3:14 AM. I had to stop writing earlier because my mom came home. Apparently Baker found her at the dance and told her everything. I guess Weird Girl is autistic or something, and she gets easily fixated on things (like me), and says a lot of things that most people find inappropriate. You think? Telling me my friend isn't going to heaven ... umm, hell, yes, I think that's inappropriate. I don't know what to think about her now. I want to hate her for what she said, but my mom said that I need to be understanding of her "condition." I'm still so mad, and I hate that I can't be mad at her. My mom didn't even care that I ran out of the dance. She said she was glad that I was home and safe, and she told me to get to bed ... but I can't sleep. I've been on the Internet all night.

I don't know much about religion. Mom and Dad stopped taking me to church when I was really little. All I can remember is having to get up early and wear a dress. When my soccer games started happening on Sunday, we all just stopped going.

I don't even know if I believe in God.

Most of the "isms" say that what you did was wrong. That you won't get to go on to whatever comes next because of it. I don't believe that, though. You were a good person. You could be a bitch sometimes, and we fought, and there was that one time you stole a chocolate bar from the convenience store ... but you were a good person. That has to count for something. It has to.

I don't know if I want to believe in a heaven, because that means there could be a hell (doesn't it?), and I can't think about you or anyone else being there. I like the idea of reincarnation. I was reading that some "isms" believe we live multiple lives, and sometimes we even get to meet up with the same spirits, which would mean that you and I might meet again ... and I like that.

It's almost 5:00 AM. I should try and sleep.

Kacey ... wherever you are, I really miss you.

Sticks

November 4th

Stones,

I'm taking guitar lessons. My mom signed me up without even asking if I wanted to go. I'm pretty sure this is her way of getting back at my dad for getting me the dog—I still don't know what to call her. And she's chewing everything I own. She completely wrecked my backpack and my favorite runners. Yes, the green Converse! AND my room smells like pee. It's not funny.

Okay, maybe it's a little funny.

My mom said she feels like I need to be doing something other than going to school and coming home. I'm sixteen; isn't that enough? She goes to work and comes home. I think she just really wants me out of the house. I've been kind of annoying, asking a lot of questions about God and religion. I think my sudden interest in religion is freaking her out. She told the OC about it, and I had to have this really awkward conversation about why I have this sudden interest in God.

It's not like I want to go and join a cult or anything. It's amazing how uncomfortable people get when the topic of religion comes up. The OC told my mom not to worry but that maybe I should have some extra-curricular outlets ... and so the guitar lessons.

At first I told her that I didn't want to take the lessons, but she looked so happy and hopeful. Anyway, I finally agreed to go. I don't know how you're going to feel about this, but I'm going to be using your guitar. You know how I told you that our moms were getting to be friends—well, that's still happening. Your mom has been phoning my mom a lot lately. When I see it's your number, I try not to answer the phone cuz ... well ... you know, it's weird. I know she wants to talk to me; it makes her feel like she might be talking to you ... maybe. I don't know. I just know I feel uncomfortable talking to her. We have nothing to say to each other. It's just awkward.

Anyway, I guess my mom told your mom about me needing to get out, and it was your mom's idea that I take guitar lessons. She told my mom that I should use your guitar ... that you would have wanted it that way. I'm not so sure you would have. I hope you're not mad about it. I'm not sure how I'm supposed to feel about our moms making plans for me together. I feel bad for your mom. I know she misses you. She asked my mom if I could babysit your little brother. I miss Owen and, I know I told you I'd look out for the little booger, but I just can't be in your house. Not without you.

   Sticks

November 7th

Stones,

I've finally come up with a name for the dog! I'm calling her Hershey, like the chocolate bar. My mom is still pretty mad that my dad got her, but at least they've stopped fighting. And on a plus note, with Hershey here, she's finally stopped complaining about my hair.

Sticks

November 9th

Dear Stones,

I'm getting good grades ... really good grades, straight A's and crap. I didn't think it was possible either, but I just brought home the first term report and I'm getting, like, 90% in all of my classes. I told you I was becoming a nerd. What's really funny is that my parents and I got called into the Dictator's office. The meeting isn't until Monday morning but my mom is all concerned about it. She asked me if I've been cheating. We had a big fight about it. I don't blame her for thinking I'm a big cheater. I wish I was cheating. It would be a lot cooler than the truth—I've become a giant geek. I pay attention in class. I get my work done. I read ahead of everyone else. I spend my lunches studying in the library. Turns out, school isn't all that hard. Maybe you really were a bad influence on me ... kidding! I just don't have a life anymore. I don't know why I have to go to Kline's office. They probably think I'm cheating, too. I don't care. I don't even care about my grades. I've stopped caring about stuff. I just feel like I'm going through the motions every day. I feel numb. Is this how you felt?

Oh, and update on Weird Girl—I haven't seen her at all since "that" night. Not in the halls, not in the lunchroom, not anywhere. It's like she's disappeared. Maybe she's scared of me now. Maybe she said what she had to say and is avoiding me now. I was kind of getting used to her. I'd never tell anyone but you this, but I kind of miss her and her strange pointy glasses.

Sticks

November 10th

Dear Stones,

I came home from school today and your guitar was just sitting on my bed. I knew my mom was going to pick it up from your mom at some point, but I wasn't really expecting it to ... I don't know ... bother me *this* much.

I walked in and it was just sitting there. Like some foreign object that didn't belong. On my bed! She could have put it anywhere else.

I dropped my backpack and walked around it like there was some force field surrounding it.

I know it's just a guitar—but it's not "just" a guitar—it's *your* guitar. It's you. It's us. It's everything.

I couldn't open it. Not yet. I didn't even want to touch it.

I finally put it in the corner of my room. It's there now.

I'm looking at it.

Sticks

November 14th

Dear Stones,

We had to fill out one of those career profile things at school today. Spend (more like waste) an hour on the computer, filling out things we like or don't like and, voila, out pops our career choice ... for life???

You should have seen how seriously everyone was taking this today. How can a computer tell us what we'll be good at? And who makes up these tests, anyway? What if it's just a bunch of computer tech nerds who were picked on in high school and, to exact their revenge, they came up with a test to mess with everyone else's life. Actually, that would be pretty funny. Doctors become actors; actors become police officers; police officers become accountants ... total anarchy. Maybe I should become a computer tech nerd just so I can do that. Except I would have to be good with computers, and we both know I'm not.

On a scale of 1 to 5, how lame did I think today's career profile was? 1 = strongly disagree and 5 = strongly agree ... I would have to go with a 7 = super strongly agree that it was super stupid and lame.

And I know what you're wondering. What did the magic fortune-telling computer say I should be? Well ... apparently I am best suited to be a Veterinarian, a Flight Attendant, or a Writer. And I know what you would say if you were here ... "Well, Sticks you did want to be a vet when we were really little." Yes, I did ... when I was eight, for about a month. I also wanted to be a marine biologist, an archeologist, and a spy. It would have been awesome if the computer popped out spy. Just because I said that I liked animals does not mean that I want to be a vet. And a Flight Attendant??? Can you imagine me in one of those tight skirts, asking if you need a pillow or want some ice with that? I guess the travel part would be exciting. I do want to travel. Okay, I get the other two, but a Writer ... come on, I hate writing ... I get that I'm doing it now, but that's only because I have to and I'm not exactly "writing," I'm just writing to you. It's like talking to you. Only it's not. I think any English teacher I've ever had would laugh if I showed them that. It's all ridiculous, anyway. I wonder how often the computer gets it right, though. Like, the percentage ... 10-15% maybe.

I wonder what it would have said for you—Singer, Writer, Artist, or something crazy like Lawyer, Professor, or Chef. I guess it doesn't matter ... and I guess I'll never know.

Kacey, I know you're gone. And I know you're not coming

back. But today, when I was filling everything out on the computer, it just kind of hit me (and now I understand why people use that expression. Because that's how it felt. Like someone hit me in the stomach) that you're not going to be here to grow up with.

We used to talk about all the stuff we were going to do together. All the places we were going to go when we graduated. What about our plans to backpack through Australia? I was going to learn to surf and you were going to play your guitar barefoot on the beach. We were going to blog and make a mini-documentary of our trip together. See how many people we could meet from around the world. What about living in the same dorm room? Living next door to one another? Having our kids play together? Growing old together? And, okay, maybe we wouldn't have done all that but ... now what? Where do I go from here ... without you?

You didn't just take your future away. You took mine, too.

Sticks

November 16th

Dear Stones,

You're not going to believe this, but I've become a teacher's aide and peer tutor. I feel like I can hear you mocking me from ... wherever you are. Anyway, that's what the meeting with the Dictator was about. Miss Baker was there and she told my parents what a pleasure I was to have in class, and that my work shows higher-level thinking or some educational crap like that. Everyone talked about me like I wasn't even there. "Sara this" and "Sara that ..."

"For a while we were worried about Sara ..."
"Sara had that outburst in the bathroom ..."
"Sara's become a model student ..."
"We feel Sara needs to be challenged."
Sara is sitting right in front of you, listening to all of you

sound like idiots.

So, basically, they're all pleased that I've dealt with the Kacey situation so well. That's what you've become to them, a "situation." They don't want to talk about what really happened. No one does. Yes, it's true that the school brought in some grief counselors at the beginning of the year, but they came and left within a week, and students only had to go see them if they wanted to.

I remember when we were in middle school and there was that girl who died of cancer. Hardly any of us knew who she was because she had been homeschooled for so long but, when she died, the whole school made the biggest deal about her. We had that assembly. They called it a celebration of life and then they named the playground after her. When you died, they didn't do anything. You became a "situation" they wanted to get through. Don't talk about what really happened. Don't "glorify" what you did. Don't let anything change. Just keep things as normal as possible.

I think that's why I bother Kline so much. Every time he looks at me, I remind him of you. I think for a while I was also a "situation" for them, but now I've become the perfect student—which makes me laugh. What I've become is this mind-numbingly boring freak who has no friends and no social life. I don't speak up in class. I don't talk to anyone. The only reason I get my work done and do what they ask is because it keeps me busy and keeps my mind off of ... "things."

The perfect student: a quiet freak with no friends, who

does her work and doesn't ask questions. Yep, I guess that's me.

Sara needs to get a life!

Sticks

*November 17*th

Dear Stones,

You never told me how silly guitar lessons were. I feel like I'm in kindergarten again. No, seriously. There's, like, a bunch of eight-year-olds in my class and they all play better than me. I can play some scales, though, and I know what a chord is. Oh, and you never told me how much it makes your fingers hurt. Seriously, my whole left hand is numb.

Every time I screw up, I feel like you're laughing at me from somewhere.

The case still has some sand in it from when we used to skip class and go to the beach. I think it smells like you— like ... I can't explain. Like wood and polish mixed with a little bit of campfire and outside air.

I found the spot where you carved your initials—KA—on the back of the neck where my left thumb sits. I feel it every time I adjust to a new chord. It's like you did that on purpose so I'd be reminded of you every time I play it. I remember the night you did it—the New Year's Eve sleepover in my basement with Loren and Drea.

My parents were having that big party upstairs. The adults were all drunk and busy playing some kind of game, Pictionary or something. No one noticed us sneaking a bottle of champagne downstairs. I remember when the cork hit the ceiling and then fell back and hit Drea in the head. We laughed for an hour after that. It didn't taste very good. But we decided to mix it with orange pop. Was that your idea? We were so paranoid that we were going to get in trouble that we drank the whole thing in about five minutes ... then we had that burping contest. That was the first time I've ever been drunk—at least, we all thought we were. We felt so grown up. Loren and Drea passed out before midnight, and then it was just you and I, sitting around, chatting about life, listening to the adults upstairs ... you took the metal wire thing from the top of the champagne bottle and turned the guitar over ...

Me: (laughing and drunk) What are you doing?

You: Carving my initials.

Me: Won't your parents be mad?

You: (shrugging) It's my guitar. And besides, I don't want to forget this night. Now, every time I look at it, I'm going to think about when I did it.

I miss you so much right now.

Sticks

November 21st

Dear Stones,

Well, the worst has happened ... brace yourself ... I've become a teacher's pet. When I agreed to do the teacher's aide thing, I didn't think about the repercussions. My parents were so proud of me when they asked, that I couldn't say no. But I should have. You should see the looks I get. They're worse than the sympathy looks.

What the hell am I doing? A year ago, I would have hated someone like me. Actual, real hatred. I would have wondered why "that" girl (me) is such a keener; I would have judged me instantly, as I'm sure half the class is doing right now. You were so much better at not judging people than I am. Remember how we used to argue about stuff like that? You would get so mad at me, and then I'd get mad at you for getting mad at me, but mostly I was just mad because

I knew you were right, and I'd feel bad. Anyway, yesterday Miss Baker asked me to collect the class tests. I could feel their judging eyes on me as I walked around the class.

"Why her?"

"Teacher's pet!"

"Miss Baker's probably taking pity on her."

"She thinks she's so special because Kacey was her best friend."

Obviously none of them actually said that stuff, but I know they were thinking it. I would have. So this is me now—straight-A student, peer tutor, teacher's pet, loner, and "that girl" who was friends with Kacey Anders.

I've changed so much since you left. Seriously. It's more than the good grades and teacher aide thing. I feel like ... like I'm starting to lose—or have already lost—a part of myself. Was that part of myself you? I'm not sure who I am without you.

Sticks

P.S. Jake said something to me. When I was collecting the tests and I got to him, he looked up, handed his test to me, and then said, "Thanks." I know it's stupid, but it was the way he said it. I didn't say anything back.

*November 24*th

Dear Stones,

I went to a concert with Loren. Well, actually, it was this
open-mic-night thing for beginner artists. My mom saw the
ad when she dropped me off at guitar lessons. She's been
so happy with me, with my grades, with my attitude lately,
that she bought me tickets to this singer-songwriter thing.
I asked Loren to go. She was really happy that I asked her.
She didn't stop talking to me the whole night—Mateo this,
Mateo that—and she apologized for not telling me about
seeing a counselor. She said it made her feel better but that
it also made her feel weak, like she couldn't get through this
on her own, and that's why she didn't want anyone to know.
I told her, "I totally get it." I feel the same way sometimes ...

Anyway, that's not what I want to tell you about. I want
to tell you that the open-mic night was really amazing. You

would have loved it. In fact ... I can't believe I did this but, on the way home, I was so excited to tell you about it that I phoned you. I did it without thinking. I realized what I was doing as soon as your voicemail picked up, and I tried to hang up before I heard your voice but I was too late. You sounded so normal, so you, so ... alive.

By the way, I can't believe that your parents still haven't canceled your phone.

I missed you tonight. I know I say that a lot, but tonight I missed you more than usual. It was totally your thing. You would have loved it. I realize I already wrote that you would have loved it but, seriously, you would have. I think you ~~are~~ were better than half the people who performed. I really missed you. It should have been you and me there instead of Loren and me.

Sticks

November 26^(th)

Dear Stones,

I got into an epic fight about you with my mom. It was a few hours ago. I took Hershey and ran out of the house and came here, to the beach.

You should have seen me. I feel like she just unlocked some anger demon. Hershey hid under the couch, whimpering. I was raging. It was like I was one of those crazy people on those trashy reality TV shows. I even threw things!!

Things between us have actually been pretty good lately, but then today I heard her talking to my grandma on the phone about how good my grades are. She said she thinks it's because you're not here anymore. But she said it in this way that totally pissed me off. Like she was right, and you always were the bad influence on me. I know she didn't mean for me to hear it and, when she saw me, she immediately tried to backtrack and make it sound like she didn't mean it that way. I said ... some pretty awful things. I feel bad but she totally deserved it. I said that she must be happy that you're finally out of my life because it's what she always wanted, and that it's her fault for trying to pull me away from you. I said other things but that really was the worst.

She's called my phone a dozen times, saying that she's sorry and that she's not mad. My dad even phoned and left a message saying how sorry she is. I know I need to go home soon but I like it here, and Hershey is having a blast, chewing on pieces of driftwood and digging random holes. Plus, I just want her to worry about me a little longer.

She did like you. She just worried about me with you sometimes. But she didn't know you like I did. No one did.

Sticks

November 30^{*th*}

Dear Stones,

You were my best friend. You were the only one who knew what my stupid parents are like, the only one I wanted to phone and talk to when I didn't want to talk to anyone. You were the only one who really understood me. You got me, you know. You never cared about the stupid crap that all those other mindless freaks in the world think about. You and I could just be. I was totally dealing with the fact that you were gone ... totally, and then, I don't know what happened.

Today I walked by your locker and I saw that silly Smurf sticker that I gave you still stuck to the top of it, and something happened. I, like, couldn't breathe. I've walked by your locker a hundred times since you've been gone, but something was different this time. It felt like one of the football guys was sitting on my chest. I had to run into the bathroom and lock myself into a stall for the rest of third block. I wasn't crying or anything like that; I just couldn't breathe. I think it was some kind of panic attack. Great, I'm having those now.

Anyway, at some point, this girl came in to use the stall next to me. I tried to be quiet but she heard me, and then she started to talk to me.

Bathroom Girl: Hey … umm … are you okay in there?
Me: I'm fine.

I was hoping she would leave but she didn't.

BG: Are you Sara Stickley?
Me: That depends. Are you the weird girl who told me my friend didn't go to heaven?
BG: No … That's awful. Who would say that?
Me: It doesn't matter.
BG: Are you sure you're okay? Do you want me to get some help or something?
Me: NO! I'm fine. Really. I just want to stay here for a while.
BG: Oh. Well, is it okay if I stay here with you?
Me: I don't want to talk.
BG: We don't have to talk.

And then things were quiet. I thought for sure she was going to get up and tell everyone that I was in the bathroom having a mental breakdown, but she didn't. After a few minutes, I couldn't take the silence.

Me: Did you know her?
BG: Sort of ... I mean, I didn't "know" her know her, but my sister did, so, kind of.

I was going to ask who her sister was, but I actually liked that I didn't know who she was. So I left it.

Me: I just miss her.
BG: I ... I lost a best friend two years ago. She moved really far away with her family. We said we'd stay in touch but that never happened. I know it's not like what happened with ... anyway, I know what it's like to miss someone. It sucks.
Me: Totally sucks.

Then two senior girls walked in and started gossiping about who was going to Winter Formal with who (or is it whom? God, I hate English) and what they were going to wear. After about five minutes, they left.

BG: I think the bell's going to go soon. I should get back to class.
Me: Thanks for ... sitting with me.
BG: No problem. Are you going to be okay?
Me: Yeah. I'll probably leave after you.

The stall door opened beside me.

Me: Thanks.
BG: No problem.

And then she was gone. I still don't have any idea who she was, but I guess it doesn't matter. It felt good to have someone other than my parents or the OC to talk to.

I really miss talking to you. We used to talk about everything ... almost everything.

Sticks

December 1ˢᵗ

Dear Kacey,

You killed yourself.
You *killed* yourself.

December 3rd

Dear Stones,

A few months ago, I was just another student. I was a "nobody." Well, okay, you're right, I wasn't a nobody, but I wasn't anyone that anyone else really cared about. I was friends with you, Drea, and Loren. I sat near the middle of the lunchroom, somewhere between the drama crew and the athletes. I was an average student who partied on the weekends, and sometimes skipped class to go to the beach with you and smoke up. Maybe I was a bit of a slacker but I was a happy slacker. When I ate lunch, sat in class, or walked down the hallway, no one cared who I was. Now they all care.

I'm no longer a nobody.

No longer average.

No longer just Sara Stickley.

I'm the girl whose best friend killed herself.

Everyone knows it ... everyone. There are Grade 9's who know who I am. I'm like a circus freak to them. Everyone, look! Feast your eyes on the girl whose best friend killed herself!

At first, everyone just kind of gave big sympathy stares. Some just looked at me with total curiosity. Others smiled, trying to get a smile out of me and make me feel better, cuz they didn't know what else to do. I'm getting fewer and fewer smiles and more looks of curiosity.

I know what they want to ask me. I've heard the whispers. I have ears but people seem to forget about that. Sometimes, like, it's a dare or just plain curiosity, someone gets the nerve to walk up to me. I usually see them coming and have enough time to either pretend I'm busy or didn't see them and leave before they get to me. I get that they want to know.

It's like when people drive by an accident and they slow down to look. They want to know what happened, how it happened, how bad it is, if anyone is hurt, and, if they're hurt, how bad it is. The funny thing is, they think they want to see it but, if they actually do see something real, like blood and bones and stuff, they turn away like they weren't expecting it and they can't believe they saw it. They might even wish they hadn't looked in the first place, because now the gruesome image is stuck with them for life.

It's the same thing with you. They think they want to know but, if they ever find out, it will haunt them. They'll fall asleep at night, dreaming up scenarios and images in their mind that probably didn't even happen ... but that I they can't help but think about, anyway.

I get that they want to know. To be completely honest, it was the first thing I wanted to know. How awful is that? I didn't know how to ask your mom. I didn't know if I should, but I didn't have to, anyway. It was one of the first things she told me. I don't know why she told me. She said it so matter-of-factly.

"Kacey swallowed almost every bottle of pills that we had ...

"She got into the bath ...

"She was still wearing her clothes ...

"The coroner believes the pills knocked her out and then she drowned."

I still can't think about that day. There are lots of rumors as to how you did it. Some are way off, but one of them is true. Besides your parents, a few cops, and some doctors, I'm the only one who knows the truth. They didn't even tell your brother Owen. Maybe one day when he's older.

How could you do that to him? Just leave him like that? You made him an only child like me. At least I never knew what it was like to have a sister, but he is going to have to live with it for the rest of his life. Did you think about that before you ...

Did you think about anything? I'm trying so hard to not be mad at you.

But I am mad!!

You killed yourself.

Sticks

You know what? No, I'm not done yet. I'm so fucking pissed off at you, you have no idea.

"See ya later." That's what you said!!

But you had to have known what you were about to do. The police and counselors all say that you must have planned it out for a few weeks, maybe even months before. And it's not just the "See ya later" that pisses me off, it was your stupid fucking text message. I still have it.

Sorry I had to leave the party early. I'm just so tired. Have fun for me.   ☺♥

Do you know how many times I've read and re-read that text? The police checked your phone. I was the last person you sent a message to. WTF? Seriously—HAVE FUN FOR ME???

How could I not have seen it?

How could I not have known what you were saying?

You knew exactly what you were doing and you didn't let me help you ... you'd never sent me a ♥ before. I just thought you were being cute. I didn't even text you back.

I remember my phone buzzing. I remember reading your

text, but I was talking to someone, I can't even remember who, and I just put my phone in my pocket.

I didn't even text you back.

Sticks

*December 4*th

Dear Stones,

I'm still mad. The worst part about being mad at you is that you're not here to be mad at and you can't argue back. I'm not going to feel guilty about being mad at you ... I'm not.

I'm not.

Sticks

❦

OC: Would you like to talk about why you haven't been writing to Kacey?

Me: Not really.

OC: Your parents are worried about you.

Me: They're always worried about me.

OC: Should they be worried about you?

Me: (rolling my eyes) You mean, should they be worried about me downing a bottle of pills, cutting my wrists, tying a noose, jumping off a bridge, pulling a trigger ...

OC: You're angry?

Me: (crossing my arms and saying nothing)

OC: Are you angry with your parents?

Me: (nothing)

OC: Are you angry with Kacey?

Me: (looking away)

OC: Are you angry with yourself?

Me: Why would I be angry with myself? Because I wasn't there when she needed me? Because I didn't respond to her text that night? Because I didn't see what she was going to do to herself? Or because I did see it but I didn't think she would do it? Because she and I weren't really best friends anymore—because I started to pull away—because I could see her drowning and, instead of throwing a life jacket, I left so she couldn't pull me down with her?

OC: Is that how you feel?

Me: Is what how I feel? Stop trying to counsel-psychoanalyze me.

OC: Do you feel that you saw her drowning?

Me: No—I don't know. She was different. She'd been different for a while.

OC: (saying nothing, waiting for me to say more)

Me: I don't know what to tell you. She just wasn't herself. If you want to know about Kacey, talk to her parents. They should know more ... they should have.

OC: Do you blame her parents?

Me: Oh, I see what you're doing. Do I blame myself? Do I blame her parents? Do I blame Kacey? Well, I don't blame anyone, okay? Life is shitty. Bad things happen.

OC: Is that how you really feel?

Me: Is what how I feel? I'm done with this. How do you feel? How do you feel about me asking how you feel? Pretty annoying, isn't it ... I'm outta here ...

OC: Sara, please sit down. I'm sorry. Please ...

Me: (sitting back down and looking out the window, wanting to be anywhere but there)

OC: Do you feel ... do you think that what happened to Kacey was just life being shitty?

Me: Obviously not. My dog peed on my bed this morning—I stubbed my toe when I was trying to clean it up—my mom found out and started to fight with my dad about taking her back to the pound again ... that's life being shitty. Is my reaction to kill myself over it? NO. Kacey killed herself. That wasn't life being shitty, that was Kacey being ... stupid and selfish and being ... Kacey ...

OC: And you're angry with her?

Me: Is that what you want me to say ... okay, here you

go. Of course I'm fucking mad at her. How could she just do that? If she was really feeling that bad, why didn't she just talk to me ... tell me ... did she think I wouldn't listen? I would have listened. I would have listened better. How could she just leave me like that? Leave me like this ...

So I cried. Finally.

The OC is pretty proud of herself. She even hugged me. Pretty sure that's against the rules but, whatever.

*December 17*th

Dear Stones,

I've been seeing the OC again ... and again, and again.
Remember her? She hasn't gone away yet and, right now,
she is making me write to you again.

I kind of stopped writing to you for the past couple
weeks. But she told me I could stop for a while. I thought
I was done with all of this. But now she says it's been long
enough and I need to finish this. Finish what? This whole
journal? It's too long. I thought I had my breakthrough. I
cried! Isn't that enough? Isn't that what they all wanted?

I was actually starting to think she wasn't all that bad, but
now that she's making me do this again ... I HATE HER all
over again. Okay, I don't hate her, but seriously ... ENOUGH
WITH THE JOURNAL, ALREADY!!

Right now, I'm sitting in her office while she taps away

on her computer. She said I can either sit in her office doing nothing or I can write to you. I can't believe my mom is paying her for this shit. I have nothing else to say to you.

You're not here.

You can't hear me.

You can't read this ... this is stupid. STUPID—HEY, OBNOXIOUS COUNSELOR WOMAN. IF YOU'RE READING THIS, I WANT YOU TO KNOW THAT I THINK THIS IS STUPID.

Sticks

*Still December 17*th

Stones,

I guess the OC actually does read some of these letters because, when she was flipping through the journal at our last appointment, she saw my note to her. I probably shouldn't have written it in capital letters. She was pretty pissed off that I wasn't taking her exercise seriously, and then she told my mom and she totally freaked out. We had a fight; my dad ended up leaving the house for a while; and I slammed a door in my mom's face. I got mad because they said that these letters were private, but I knew she was reading them. I'm the one who should be angry. Invasion of privacy, much?!

"Her exercise"—nice to know that's what this is to her. I lost my best friend and she's mad that I'm not following her fucking exercise properly. I love that everyone has an opinion about me. They all think they know what I'm going through, how I should be feeling, what I should be doing. Everyone's got an opinion, but no one cares about mine.

I just want things to go back to normal. As normal as they can be. It's not that I want to forget about you. I'll never forget. I just can't stand the way people tiptoe around me anymore. Everyone's worried that they're going to say the wrong thing or do something that will upset me. Like the other day in English, we started a Shakespeare unit. You know how I hate Shakespeare. I can never understand anything that guy writes. I don't understand why they are still teaching this. It's not like we even talk like that anymore. Shakespeare was your thing, and now I'm going to have to suffer through it without you.

Anyway, we're doing *Romeo and Juliet*, and when Baker started talking about the themes and giving an overview of the play, she said something about their deaths at the end and mentioned suicide—and then she paused. It was super awkward. Not only did she pause, but she looked up at me, I guess to see if I was upset, and the whole class turned around and looked at me, too. I think everyone was waiting to see how I would react. If I would react. If I'm going to have some kind of breakdown—they're all waiting for it. When will Sara finally lose it? Tick-tock, tick-tock ... It's not going to be during *Romeo and Juliet*. It's not like the end of the play is coming as a surprise. Even a Shakespeare hater like me knows how that story ends. The whole world knows how it ends.

What did she think? It was the first time I was going to

hear about it?! Surprise, Romeo and Juliet don't get to live happily ever after. Two star-crossed lovers take their lives— duh, that's why it's a tragedy not a comedy.

We have a quiz on literary definitions tomorrow.

Tragedy

1. a play / novel / literary composition dealing with tragic events that has an unhappy ending.

2. a drama in which the protagonist is destined through a flaw of character or conflict to be overcome by social and/or psychological circumstances, usually ending in disaster or downfall.

3. an event causing great suffering, destruction, and distress.

I'm going to ace that quiz.
Sticks

December 20th

Dear Stones,

Today was the last day of school before winter vacation. It was a pretty typical last day—movies, games, candy canes, and one science test. Why is there always that one grinchy teacher who is so against the holidays and fun that they have to give a test on the last day? I don't get it. Does his Christmas suck so much that he has to bring ours down, too? Maybe it does. Now I just feel bad for the guy. Maybe he sits at home, alone, no family, no tree, no lights, no presents ... that would suck.

Anyway, that's not why I am writing to you ... I have to tell you what happened at the Winter Wonderland Show. Nothing unusual with the show—Mr. Kline was dressed up as Santa again. The choir came out and sang all the usual songs. Mary and Joseph led the politically correct cultural parade across the stage, complete with Jewish menorahs, Chinese dragons, Elves, etc ... and everyone in the audience singing "Feliz Navidad" as they marched. That was all pretty normal ... an abnormal normal, but nothing out of the ordinary as far as the show was concerned. What I have to tell you about happened with me.

I was sitting at the back, trying to avoid everyone as usual, when Hockey Jake came and sat down beside me. There were lots of other seats but he came and sat beside *me*. We smiled awkwardly, and then the lights dimmed and the show began. After a few minutes, he leaned in and started whispering ...

Jake: Mr. Kline looks ridiculous in that Santa suit.

Me: (shocked he was talking to me) Totally.

Jake: Is your family doing anything over Christmas?

Me: No. We usually all go to my grandma's house. My mom's side of the family comes for dinner—crazy drunk uncles, annoying cousins ... We play some lame family games, open presents, eat turkey ... (At this point, I realized that I was talking too much) ... you know how it is. How about you?

Jake: Same. Although this year I got invited to a select hockey camp and I leave on the day after Christmas—for a week in Russia.

Me: Russia?

Jake: Yeah.

Me: That sounds cool.

Jake: It should be. I mean we don't really get to go anywhere besides the hotel and the arena but, still ...

At that point, a teacher came over and shushed us so we couldn't talk anymore. I don't know what to think about it. I mean, it wasn't a huge deal but it was kind of a small deal. He talked to me. And then, when the show let out and we got up to leave, he turned as we were going out and wished me a Merry Christmas. I don't know if he's just taking pity on me because of the whole "you" thing, or if he's actually trying to talk to me. I don't know what to think. After I got home I creeped him on FB. There are some pretty cute pictures of him on there, mostly of him playing hockey. I'm not friends with any of his friends. We don't really have that much in common. I don't know why he's talking to me ... and now I have to wait all vacation to see him again. This is the kind of stuff you should be here for.

Sticks

December 22ⁿᵈ

Dear Stones,

   I just saw Weird Girl again!! I was out shopping at the mall (well, not really shopping, just tagging along while my mom shopped for Christmas presents) and there "she" was. She was wearing a green Santa hat and ringing one of those bells to collect money for the poor. She looked different out of school—normal. I'm still pissed at her for what she said about you but not as much as I was. And now that I know she's got real issues, I feel kind of bad for her. My mom saw me looking, and she thought I was looking because I wanted to give money, so she gave me five bucks and told me to go and put it in the bucket. Talking to Weird Girl again was the last thing I wanted to do, but it was for the poor so I didn't really have a choice.

Me: Umm, hi. Here (putting the money in).

WG: Hi. Thanks.

Me: (turning to leave)

WG: I'm sorry ... about what I said. My dad said that even if we think some things, we shouldn't always say them.

Me: (stopping ... turning back)

WG: I've never known anyone who has died before. Well, my grandpa on my mom's side died two years ago, but I had only met him once when I was really little. He smelled like cigarettes and dirty socks.

Me: That's okay.

WG: Why did she do it? I'm sorry. I'm not supposed to ask that.

Me: It's okay—I don't know.

WG: I'm sure she's in heaven.

Me: I'm not (but I whispered it so she didn't hear me).

WG: What?

Me: Nothing. Do you get paid to do this?

WG: No. It's volunteer. My dad makes me do it every year. This is the first time I get to do it all by myself. He's always worried someone will rob me.

Me: Who would do that?

WG: It happens. It happened to a woman at the other end of the mall last year. But she was standing by the outside door, and my dad said that I would be okay here, because it's inside the mall and there are lots of people and security guards around.

Me: (nodding ... awkward silence) Well ... I hope that doesn't happen to you. (I realize that was a stupid thing to say but I didn't have anything else.) I better get going. Merry Christmas.

WG: Thanks. You, too.

She actually didn't seem that weird outside of school. I mean, I can tell there is something "off" with her, but it's not as obvious outside of school. It's like she blends in better in the real world.

I can't stop thinking about her. About why she's so interested in you. And I think it's because she can't understand why you would do what you did. She has actual problems. I know we sometimes think life hasn't been fair to us, but life really hasn't been fair to her, and you had it all. You didn't have any problems or things to deal with—not like autism, or a bad family, or like the people who live on the streets, or like the starving kids in Africa—you were normal. You had people in your life who loved you. I think she just wants to know what made you believe that life was so bad you couldn't be here anymore.

She just can't understand why.

Sticks

December 23rd

Dear Stones,

I finally went over to your house. I didn't want to go but my mom made me go with her. She said that this will be their first year without you, and we need to do whatever we can to make it better. Make it better. I know what you'd say if you were here. Make it better than what? The truth is that Christmas at your house always sucked. That's why you usually came to mine almost every day of the holidays—not that my family is that much better. I remember last year when you told me that the real "F" word during the holidays is "family." You said that Christmas was just a time for everyone to get together for a couple of days and pretend to be happy and like each other. But no matter how bad your family's Christmas usually is, I'm sure this year will be worse.

Anyway, that's why we went to drop off some Christmas baking. It's the first time I've been in your house since ... you know; I can't even remember when the last time was. Was it ... was it "the fight?" I think it was.

You weren't at school ... again. The teachers gave me some homework to give to you. When I came over, your mom told me you were in one of your "moods" and were up in your room, listening to music. She said that she had tried to get you to go to school that day but you weren't feeling well again.

Was that a sign?

When I walked in, you were happy to see me. I gave you your homework and you said ...

You: I see the school has you doing their dirty work for them.

Me: Where do you want me to put it?

You: On my desk with the rest of it.

Me: Why didn't you come today?

You: I'm sick ... cough ... cough ... can't you tell?

Me: I can't believe your mom fell for that.

You: They believe whatever I tell them. You just have to know what to say to get them to leave you alone. *How was your day?* Fine. *How was school?* Boring, as usual. *What did you do?* Little of this, little of that. Then my dad grabs the paper and leaves; my mom goes into the kitchen and does mom stuff; my brother leaves to play with his Lego; and I come up here and listen to music. It's the same whether I go to school or not. We're all just going through the motions, Sticks.

Was that a sign?

Me: I miss you when you're not there.
You: You just miss having someone to distract you from work. Besides, you still have Loren and Drea to keep you company.
Me: Not the same.
You: I know. I'll be there tomorrow. (But you weren't. You stayed home sick again.)
Me: What do you do here all day?
You: Write songs, mostly.
Me: Anything new?
You: Yes. Want to hear it?
Me: Yeah.

And then I sat down and you played a song about two friends going down to the water at night. Something about how life was short but summer days were long ... Was that a sign?

You: Hey, why don't you skip school with me tomorrow? We can go to the beach, write some songs together.
Me: I can't. Last time, the school phoned my house and my mom grounded me for a week. Remember?
You: Well, who cares? It'll be worth it.
Me: I can't. And you need to go to school.
You: Why? It's a huge waste of time.

Me: And sitting up here alone, in your room, is better how?

You: No one asked you.

Me: Don't get mad. I just don't understand why ...

You: Because I don't feel like it. I'd rather sleep and play music. I don't need to go to school to be the next singing idol.

Me: That's your plan?

You: Shut up. You thought it was a good plan before.

Me: Yeah, when you were going to school.

You: You don't think I can do it?

Me: That's not what I said ...

You: You don't think I'm good enough.

Me: No, I do ...

You: GET OUT.

Me: Stones, I didn't mean ...

You: I don't care. GET OUT. I don't need you. I don't need anyone.

And then you shut the door in my face. Your mom told me not to take it personally, that you had been in a bad mood for a few days.

Was that all a sign? Of course it was. Why didn't I see it then?

I'm pretty sure that was the last time I was in your house. I didn't see you as much after that. I think you stayed mad at me for a while. I was mad at you, too. I just thought you were being a bitch ... I didn't know you were going through other things ... I didn't know.

Apparently, you hid it well from everyone. Your mom told me that she knew you weren't yourself, but she thought it was just you being a moody teenager. I asked her about you—when my mom and I went over.

I just need to understand ... and I don't.

I asked her if she saw anything. If she suspected anything. My mom got upset when I brought it up. She said we were there for Christmas, not for that. But your mom said it was all right. That she had wanted to talk to me about it. We talked for over an hour. I felt like you were there, listening the whole time. I kept waiting for you to walk down the stairs and join us ... yell at us ... tell us to stop talking about you. But you never did.

She told me that the doctors think you were suffering from depression or some kind of mental health disorder. Disorder—it just sounds so medical, so cold, so ... psycho ward.

The moodiness, the missed school, the sleeping, some of the things you wrote in your journal ... that it all made sense and fit with depression. But ... I don't know if I believe that.

They read your journal. They dissected it page by page, word by word, letter by letter, ripping you open and taking out your insides to see what was making you tick. And somewhere, hidden amongst the song lyrics and absent-minded thoughts, they found a depression demon that was clouding your thoughts, making you do / say / think things that weren't true.

I don't know ... I think it's a copout. Maybe you were suffering from depression and maybe you weren't. I think your mom needs to believe you were. I think everyone needs to believe you were. That it was the depression demon's fault ... and not our own. That you were sick, and it wasn't you calling the shots and pulling the strings. It was something else. Something sinister. We need to believe it because it gives us an answer. And we all need an answer. So we give ourselves one to make it all feel better. But the truth is, we'll never know why because only you ~~know~~ knew ... and you can't tell us.

By the way, if you're wondering, I didn't get to see your brother. Apparently he was at a sleepover. Your mom said he's happier when he's playing at a friend's house because he thinks less about you. Your dad wasn't around, either. She didn't say where he was.

Merry Christmas.

Sticks

December 26th

Stones,

As usual, the holidays suck. Christmas dinner was typical. It started all nice and formal but, as the night went on (and the drinking went on), it evolved into family reminiscing, which inevitably led to family fighting and fa la la la la ... I hid in the corner by the tree, reading a new book I got in my stocking and trying to ignore the world. You were right about the "F" word.

As I was reading, out of the corner of my eye, I could see a group of my younger cousins whispering and daring one another to do something. Finally Emma, the oldest, came over...

Emma: Is it true that your best friend jumped off a bridge?
Me: Where did you hear that?

Emma: Some kids at school.

Me: It's not true. Now go away.

Emma: How'd she do it, then?

Me: None of your business.

Emma: Do you even know?

Me: (not answering, trying to read and ignore her)

Emma: I bet you don't know.

Me: Get outta here.

Emma: (turning to her siblings) Told ya she doesn't know.

At that point, my Aunt Carolyn came over and told them to leave me alone. She apologized and said that she had told them all to be nice and not bother me this Christmas. Which is a change, because usually I'm the one left to babysit everyone else.

Even from my little reading corner, I could hear all the adults whispering about me—my mom trying to reassure everyone that I'm fine and coping well. She left out the part where she discovered my search history on the computer and totally freaked out the day before.

I'm usually really good about erasing it, but I guess the one time I forgot is the one time she finds it. Typical. Now she's all worried about me again. I have another appointment with the OC in two days. She wasn't supposed to have any appointments over the holidays but she's made a special exception for me. Sarcastic "Yay!"

It wasn't like I was researching how to commit suicide or anything ... although she's acting like I was. It started with me looking up bipolar disorder, and that led to a link about teenage depression, and that led to another link about teen suicide (one of the five leading causes of death among teens, the first being accidents), and then I was on a page about famous suicides through history: Kurt Cobain (knew about that one), Sylvia Plath (knew about that one, too), Vincent van Gogh, Ernest Hemingway and his granddaughter Margaux Hemingway (lots of depression demons in that family), Virginia Woolf ... and so many more ... all writers and artists, kind of like you.

The pages all linked to other places, some that showed their work, fan sites, and some that listed how they committed suicide ... and I think that was the page that my mom found, so, of course, she had a mini heart attack and booked an appointment for me with the OC right away.

I told her it wasn't what she was thinking. How could she think that? I was just ... I don't know ... curious. It didn't start out with me looking for that information—it kind of just happened.

I can't believe all the ways people have done it. I am kind of wondering why you chose to do "it" the way you did. If you researched "it?" Of course you did, because you're you and you never did things halfway. That's one thing people always said about you ... "If Kacey wants to do something, there's no stopping her. She'll do it." You wanted to learn how to play guitar and then, that same year, you won the school's talent show, singing and playing your own song.

You wanted to be in the play and you inevitably got the lead.
Anything you wanted ... you got it. Congratulations to you.
   Sticks

December 28th

Dear Stones,

I guess I said all the right things because the OC has cleared me. I'm not crazy. She told my mother that this is a normal reaction, and I'm displaying normal behavior for a person who is "dealing with the loss of a friend from such a sudden and tragic circumstance."

So there, Mom—I'm normal.

Abnormally yours,

Sticks

January 1st

Dear Stones,

The craziest thing just happened. I was in my room just hanging with Hershey and practicing a little guitar, when I heard my computer ping. I must have left my FB chat on (no one usually wants to talk to me, anyway) but someone was trying to message me...

Jake: Hey Sara! You around?

Hi

Jake: Hi!

Aren't you supposed to be in Russia?

Jake: I am! Today's my last day. We leave tomorrow.

How was it?

Jake: Really cool. I got my ass kicked but it was fun. Shouldn't you be out for New Year's Eve?

Didn't feel like it.

Jake: I get it. Hasn't really been a year to celebrate.

Jake: Sorry.

It's okay. You're right. It wasn't.

Jake: Did you have a good Christmas?

It was okay. You?

Jake: Same.

It just turned midnight.

Jake: Looks like you spent New Year's Eve with me!

I guess I did =)

Jake: Sorry, I have to go. Game in an hour.

That's okay. Have fun.

Jake: Happy New Year, Sara!

Happy New Year, Jake!

And that was it. Not sure what I am supposed to think about this. I mean, he messaged with me, which means he must have been thinking about me, right?! And I was so lame. Actually being home by myself for New Year's Eve. He must think I'm a total loser.

"Looks like you spent New Year's Eve with me!"—what was that? How am I supposed to take that? Am I just being a "girl" and overanalyzing everything? Does he like me?

I can hear my parents coming up the stairs to wish me a Happy New Year. Gotta go.

Oh, and Happy New Year!

Sticks

*January 9*th

Stones,

I'm sitting in the medical room at school, waiting for my mom to come and get me.

I was hoping to start this year fresh. Maybe come back from winter break with some degree of normality. I hate how the start of every new year comes with some false hope that things could be different somehow. I didn't make any resolutions or anything, I just ... I don't know, new year = new me. Stupid.

I was actually excited for school to start up again. And yes, that might have had something to do with the fact that I was going to see Jake for the first time since messaging with him. But when I saw him in English, he just smiled at me and said, "Hey," and that was it. We never talked about New Year's Eve ... not that there was anything to talk about, I guess.

Anyway, back to me in the medical room. So, today we were dissecting frogs in science class. Not something I was really looking forward to, but also not something that I thought was going to bother me. A few students opted out of the dissection for personal / religious beliefs, or simply because they thought it would be "gross." I didn't really think about it.

Mr. Ross set us up with lab partners. I was partnered with Hanna Barton, the girl who won female athlete of the year last year. I think she's some kind of soccer star. She's seems nice, a little intense, and she was really excited about getting our frog.

So we got the frog carcass—where do they get these things, anyway? Do you think that the frog woke up from his froggy sleep one day and knew this was the day that he was going to be plucked from his swamp, killed, and then served up on a metal sheet for some teenagers to cut him open? Anyway ... the first thing we had to do was pin it down on the tray. Hanna asked me to do it while she started to sketch its body on our lab report.

I had to put the thing on its back and pin the arms and legs down so it was ready for us to slice open. I did that with no problem. But then I looked at it. All splayed out like that. And I started to feel ... I don't know how to describe it. The room started to feel like it was closing in. Everything started to sound muffled. And then it passed. And for a few minutes I felt okay again.

But then it came time for us to cut it open. Hanna wanted

to do it. She took the scalpel they gave us and started to cut a line up ... I can't even write about it. It's starting to make me feel sick again. And that's what happened. I got sick. I couldn't control it.

I just threw up right there.

In the middle of class.

In front of everyone.

The room closed in again.

And I woke up here.

So, that happened.

I've never passed out before. Mr. Kline came in and said they were thinking about calling an ambulance. Can you imagine? That's the last thing I need. To be taken away from the school in an ambulance. I'm already probably what everyone is talking about ... again! I convinced him that I was fine and to let my mom come and get me.

I just can't believe I threw up in school. And it hit me so fast. One minute I was fine, and then BLAH. That's never happened to me before. EVER.

It was you. Something about the frog lying there like that. Helpless. Ready to be cut open. It had to be you.

Loren popped in to see if I was okay. She said I'm all anyone is talking about. Apparently I threw up on Hanna's new runners. And I'm sure Jake's heard about it by now. I think he's friends with her.

So much for a new year = new me.

Sticks

January 10ᵗʰ

Dear Stones,

My mom made me go to school today. I wanted to stay home, and she nearly let me, but then she phoned the OC about what happened, and the OC told her that the best thing for me to do was get back to school and continue with my normal activities.

Continue with my normal activities?? Does she forget what school is like?

When my mom dropped me off, I almost took off, but then I heard you in my head, telling me that I couldn't hide forever and to just get it over with. Pull the band aid!

Ya, I should have just left when I had the chance. I didn't even go to science, because Mr. Ross thought it was best if I wrote a research paper about frogs in the library until the dissections were over. Weird Girl was there.

WG: You threw up during school yesterday.

Me: Yep.

WG: In the middle of class. With everyone watching.

Me: Yep.

WG: That's gross.

Me: Yep.

WG: Are you okay today?

Me: (nodding) I think so.

WG: Good, because I don't want to see you throw up, and my class is in the library for the rest of the block. If I see someone throw up it makes me throw up. And I had oatmeal and blueberries for breakfast, so that would be gross.

And then she left. The funny thing is, talking with her was actually the best part of my day. I saw Jake in the hallway, but he was with a group of his friends and, when they saw me, he just turned his back and they all started laughing. At lunch I went to buy a drink in the cafeteria but, as soon as I walked in, Drea pointed, said something, and then the whole middle table started laughing and pretending to vomit. And that's pretty much how the rest of my day went. Pointing. Laughing. Staring. Whispers. I guess I should be looking on the bright side. It wasn't about you this time.

Sincerely,

Sara Spew—that's what someone called me today.

P.S. At this very moment, Hershey is digging her way through my laundry basket, looking for socks to chew. I wish you could see her. She's pretty funny. And right now, she's the only one in my life who doesn't look at me like I'm some weirdo or charity case.

January 24th

Dear Stones,

I know I haven't written in a while. I've been dealing with stuff, trying to act like things are normal, which they almost are. Most of the school has stopped talking about the "Frog Incident." Some kid accidentally started a mini fire in the Home Ec room, and now that's all anyone is talking about. Nothing major. There was only minor damage and no one was hurt but, thankfully, it pulled everyone's focus off me for a while.

Right now, I'm in a bit of a rush. I'm sitting in the waiting room of the counselor's office, trying to write so I have something to show her. She told me that from now on, she would look but not read. As long as I had something on paper, she would be satisfied. I feel like I'm trying to get my homework done five minutes before class.

I just grabbed this pamphlet on the five stages of grief. Let's see ...

DENIAL. Been there, done that. When Drea phoned and told me, I thought she was playing some cruel prank. Then my mom told me and I think ... I think I told her to shut up, not in an angry way, but in an I-can't-believe-you type of way. It all gets kind of fuzzy, but I remember going to your house and sitting on the front porch while my mom talked to your mom. Even when I saw your mom sobbing, I still didn't believe it. Even when she told my mom how she found you ... I still didn't believe it then. I'm not sure when it got real. I'm still not sure it has.

ANGER. I'm sure my mom would say that I've been through this stage. She probably thinks I'm still going through it. I guess I have been angry, with Drea, with Weird Girl, with my mom, with the obnoxious counselor ... with you.

BARGAINING. Really, bargaining? I don't know who I'd bargain with or what I'd bargain for. The pamphlet says it's like when someone gets cancer and they bargain with God to get better or to let their loved one get better. How can I bargain with someone who chose death?

DEPRESSION. Uh, no ... I'm not so upset that I feel like the world is coming to an end or anything. I'm not you.

ACCEPTANCE. You're gone. I "accept" it. The OC is waving me in.

Sticks

P.S. I can't wait for this to all be over ... will it ever be?

February 4th

Dear Stones,

I've officially made a bathroom friend. I'm really not sure what to call her. I don't even know what she looks like. I know it's weird but I kind of like her. After the first time we talked, I snuck away to the bathroom a few times and just waited for her. I sat in that bathroom stall, waiting for hours. I'm sure all of my teachers think I have some kind of stomach problem. Although, after the whole "frog" thing, no one questions when I ask to go!

One day, after I had been waiting for two blocks, I thought she came into the stall next to me. I really thought it was her, so I said, "Hey." Then, whoever it was answered, "Hey," so I just started talking, about how happy I was that she finally came back, how I had waited in the stall for her to come ... I must have talked for two minutes nonstop before whoever it was flushed the toilet, laughed, and called me a "freak." Which I have to admit I kind of am. I stopped waiting in the stall after that. I still snuck away to the bathroom every now and then, hoping she'd be there, but she never was.

I was starting to think that I had made her all up. Like maybe she was a figment of my imagination or a ghost or something. But then yesterday, when I went to the bathroom—to actually go to the bathroom—she was there, in the stall next to me. I know it was her because she talked to me first. She just asked if I was Sara Stickley. I didn't think it was her but I answered back anyway, cuz I was hoping it was her ... and it was.

I told her how I'd waited in the bathroom for her a few times. She thought that was weird and we both laughed about it. Then I told her about how I talked to someone I thought was her, and how I was starting to think she was a ghost, and we laughed again.

It felt good to laugh.

We couldn't talk for long because she was working on a project with a group in her class, but she agreed to come and meet with me again during second block tomorrow. She asked if I wanted to meet her some other place, face to face. I couldn't answer. I don't know why I couldn't, why I didn't. It's just that ... I don't know what she looks like, and I like that I don't know. I don't have to see her in the halls or in class or at lunch. Anyway, I didn't have to answer, because she said she understood and that she'd meet me in the bathroom any time. And that's why I like her. She gets me. Like I said, I know it's weird, but talking with her is as close as I've felt to normal in a really long time.

    Sticks

February 10th

Stones,

I think you're haunting me. Not in the ghostly "boo" sense of the word but, like, I can feel you sometimes.

All the places we used to go together. Places we'd hang out, like our ocean spot, or the 7-Eleven on the corner where we used to get bags of five-cent candy and Slurpees almost every Friday after school. You'd always buy sour keys and blue whales and then drop a blue whale into your Slurpee. Then, once you slurped every last drop from the bottom of your cup, you'd harpoon the whale with your straw and eat it last.

The frozen yogurt place in the mall food court.

Pages—your favorite bookstore. I'd always find you curled up in the classics section with some huge novel you could barely lift.

Sips—the café with that hot artsy coffee barista who you loved to flirt with but was way too old for you.

The movie theater.

I feel you everywhere. It's like you're still here.

Sometimes I can look at a chair you used to sit in, and I think I can see you there ... or a faint outline of you. Sometimes I swear I can hear your voice or your laugh coming from somewhere, and sometimes I even look to see if you're there. It's like a reflex I can't control.

And we have conversations. Sometimes out loud. Sometimes just in my head. But I talk to you, like you're still here. And I know you're not, and I know you can't talk back, but we still talk because I know exactly what you'd say if you were here.

You: Maybe I am haunting you ... Ouuuuooooooo ...

Me: You think I'm crazy?

You: I think you miss me.

Me: You think?!

You: You don't have to get snarky.

Me: I know you're not actually here.

You: I know you know. But I like that you feel me sometimes. And that you see my outline ... the *evanescence* of me.

Me: You would use some fancy word for it.

You: Uh, you're the one imagining this conversation, so actually, you're the one who thought up the word.

Me: Whatever. Only you would point that out.

You: True. I wish you weren't so bitter with me.

Me: I'm not.

You: You are.

Me: I'm trying not to be.

You: What is it, Sticks? What do you want to ask me?

Me: Were you really sick?

You: If that's what they're saying.

Me: That's not really an answer.

You: I wish I could give you a better one.

Me: Me, too.

I don't know what bothers me more, the idea that you're haunting me, and that I can see, hear, and sense you all around me ... or the idea that you might stop, and I won't see your outline or hear your laugh anymore ... that one day you'll just be gone.

Sticks

*February 13*th

Dear Stones,

I'm trying out for the track team. Can you believe it? I feel like I can hear you making fun of me again. I didn't really have a choice. Ever since my mom found all that depression/ suicide stuff I was looking up on the computer, she's been worried about me. Even though the OC told her that things are fine, they both agreed that I should be doing more with my time.

My options were:

Yearbook Committee—I'm already a big enough loser, thank you.

Spirit Squad—Even my mom agreed that wasn't for me.

Drama—No way I'm going up on stage; I'd rather be ... never mind.

Sports—I used to like cross-country and, besides, I figure

I can go out for the team, and when I don't make it, my mom will feel bad and leave me alone. Tryouts are next week, so I'll let you know how that goes.

I'd write more but Hershey's nuzzling into me like she wants to go out. She's getting bigger and bossier. The other morning, I woke up and she was under the covers with me. I didn't even feel her crawl in. My mom wants her to sleep in the laundry room, but she cries when she's alone, so I usually go down and sneak her up when my parents go to bed. Truth is, I kind of like having her beside me at night.

Okay, she's getting really pushy, and last time she peed on my favorite hoodie, so I better take her. And yes, the hoodie I'm talking about used to be your favorite purple hoodie, but you never asked for it back, so ...

Sticks

February 17th

Dear Stones,

Today's been a crappy day. The weather sucks. It's been super dark out all day, and it hasn't stopped raining since last night. Normally, I like the rain but, today ... today, I can't stop thinking about you. Sometimes it's like this. Some days I don't really think about you too much, and others, like today ... I can't stop thinking about you.

When you left, I was still at that party. I mean, I was there when you left the actual party, but I think I was still there when you, like, "really" left. I heard the police tell your mom something about your presumed time of death. And if it really was between 1 and 2 AM, then I was partying and having fun when you died. I know I couldn't have known what you were doing but, still ... I was partying.

I walked home with Loren, Drea, Adam, Mateo, and

Rebecca. I remember it was Drea who convinced us to stay out longer. Take the long way home. She was in a fight with her parents and didn't want to go home until she knew they were in bed.

We walked through the tennis courts near your house. We were laughing and throwing empty beer cans over the nets in the court. We made a game of it and wanted to see who could throw the farthest. Was that when you were killing yourself? Were you dying? Were you already dead?

I remember sneaking into the house so I wouldn't wake up my parents—and so they wouldn't find out that I'd been drinking. I checked my phone and texted with Loren about Mateo. Texted with Drea about her parents. Then I fell asleep.

I woke up when Drea phoned. I was mad that she was calling because I still felt sick and I just wanted to sleep. I almost didn't pick it up.

She'd heard from someone who heard from someone that there were police at your house, and that they had put a body in the back of an ambulance.

"Everyone is saying that Kacey is dead."

That's what she said.

That's how I found out.

My mom came into my room and ripped the phone out of my hand. But it was too late. I think I got mad, and all I kept yelling was for her to shut up and that it wasn't true. Over and over again, I kept saying the same thing. My mom told me that you had committed suicide. Committed suicide. She had just gotten off the phone with your dad. He asked if she could come over to be with your mom, because he was taking Owen to get some ice cream.

I went with my mom to your house. Your mom was sitting on the porch outside. We never went into the house. Our moms just sat on the porch and talked.

I remember sitting on the steps, thinking about how tired and hungry I was. Your mom was crying but she was also weirdly calm. Tears were falling but it wasn't like she was sad, there was, like, no emotion to her voice at all. It was weird. I listened to her telling my mom about how she found you. How you looked like you were just sleeping. I don't remember being sad or upset or any of that. Maybe that's what she felt—nothing.

When your dad came back with Owen, I asked my mom if we could go out for dinner. I do remember feeling guilty for wanting to eat. Like maybe the right reaction was for me to be crying in a ball on my bed or something. But I was hungry. I hadn't eaten anything since the night before.

We went for burgers. My dad watched a football game on the big TV. I don't remember talking about anything. I remember I had only eaten about half my burger, when I asked if we could go home. I'm pretty sure my parents weren't done eating, but we all left anyway.

I wanted to have a bath, but then I thought about you. I couldn't stop seeing you. I had a shower instead, and I remember that I couldn't stop thinking about you, so I kept turning the hot water up, until all I could think about and feel was the heat turning my skin bright red.

I went into my room and checked my phone. I had over

a hundred messages from different people. My FB page was covered with notes and questions asking if it was true/ what had happened / if I had talked to you before / how was I? I just couldn't deal with any of it then, so I turned off my computer, put my phone on silence, and went to bed. I'm not completely sure, but I think it was that night that I scrolled through all of our past texts to each other. I think I fell asleep right after that.

I still think about that night a lot. I wonder what would have happened if I had asked you to stay.

The truth is ... the truth is ... I didn't want you to stay that night. You were being a total downer and, when you left, I remember that I felt ... not happy, but relieved. With you at the party, I wasn't having any fun, because I felt like I needed to stay with you, keep you happy and involved ... I was drunk but I can remember you saying that you thought you should go—and I said, "Okay." I didn't say that I wanted you to go but, I think, when I agreed you should go, you knew that I didn't really want you to stay. It's just that ... you weren't any fun to be around. I never knew if you were going to be in a good mood or not. And in order to keep you happy, I was always careful about what I said, and I tried to do everything you wanted to do ... and it was exhausting. I wanted to party with Loren and Drea without you. I wanted you to go home that night. I just wanted to have fun. And now I just feel like the worst friend in the world. The OC said that it was natural to feel guilty. That when something like this happens, we all feel like we could have done something more. What if it's not something I didn't do but something

I did? I shouldn't have said, "Okay," when you wanted to leave. I was basically telling you to go. I should have told you to stay. I should have wanted you to stay.

I don't know why I'm writing this. I feel like I had a point when I started, but now I don't know what it was.

Sticks

P.S. It's still raining.

February 22nd

Dear Stones,

So I made the track team! WTF ... I know! I wasn't planning on trying hard or anything but, once I started running, it just felt so good. I wasn't thinking about anything or anyone, just how the cool spitting rain felt on my face. At some point, I was lapping other runners and they had to yell at me to stop, because I just wanted to keep going.

The coach asked why I had never tried out before—I don't know. He said he was going to put me in the distance events, and he seemed pumped about winning the city championship this year. Whatever, like I care. My mom's happy, which means she's backing off a bit. There is no way I'm going to let her know that I actually like it.

Oh, and guess who is also on the track team? Hockey Jake! Apparently, he's a really good runner, but I think it's in the sprinting events. We smiled at each other once when I ran by. I think he was really surprised to see me running. He's not the only one.

Sticks

March 3rd

Stones,

I just got back from a party. It was at Hanna's house. I never thought I would go to a party at her house—especially after the whole throwing up on her shoes thing. I apologized for wrecking her shoes and told her that I'd buy her some new ones, but she said it was no big deal and that her parents already got her a bunch of new pairs. Then she asked me if I threw up because of the frog or because of you. She didn't actually say "you" but I knew what she was asking. I told her that I didn't really know why it happened ... and I still don't.

Anyway, it's not like we're friends but we talk a lot more. I think it's some kind of athlete respect thing. She invited the whole track team over to her place and, since I'm on the team ... I wouldn't have gone but it was Jake who told me about it. And even with him telling me, I still wasn't going to go, but then I talked with my bathroom friend about it and she told me, "You so totally have to go." So, I went.

It was strange. Not the house, just being at the party. Everyone was pretty cool. At first, a few people gave me the "you're the friend of that girl" look but, as the night went on, everyone just did their own thing and no one really noticed me. I mean, they noticed me. I wasn't just standing in the corner by myself, but they didn't notice me in "that" way. I was one of them. Me. A jock. As crazy as that is, it wasn't why I felt strange at the party. It was just being there. With people. The music. The alcohol. I haven't been to a party since ... that night. I started to feel uncomfortable and I was going to leave, but then Jake saw me and pulled me outside.

Jake: What's up? Are you okay?
Me: I hate that question.
Jake: Sorry. You must be getting it a lot, hey?
Me: It's all anyone ever asks me.
Jake: What's your favorite hockey team?
Me: (confused) What?
Jake: I bet no one's asked you that lately.
Me: Noooo, they have not.
Jake: So?
Me: Ummm ...
Jake: You don't watch hockey, do you?
Me: Not really. Sorry.
Jake: Don't be sorry.

I think I must have shivered at this point because ...

Jake: Are you cold? Here.

AND he actually took off his jacket and gave it to me. I kept waiting for some light 80's music to play or for John Cusack to come walking out with a ghetto blaster above his head.

Okay, John Hughes / classic 80's movie marathon week may have skewed my view on high school romance.

Me: Ummm ... thanks. (And then I laughed a little.)
Jake: What?
Me: I've just never had a guy give me his jacket before.
Jake: Oh. Kind of cheesy, huh?
Me: A little. But it's nice.
Jake: So, you didn't want to be at the party anymore?
Me: No ... it's just that ... I haven't been to a party since ...

But I just couldn't tell him the real reason. I don't know why.

Me: ... it's just been a long time.
Jake: That's okay. I get it.

Then he ... it's going to sound strange, but he grabbed my hand and just held it while we walked. At first I was going to pull mine away, but it felt kind of nice to have a hand to hold. Nothing else happened. I swear. We just held hands and kept walking around the house for a while. I'm not sure how long. At some point, a group of people came out of the house to smoke up or something, so we let go and went back in to the party. I don't know what to think about it ... about him. Boys are strange. First the New Year's chat, then he practically ignores me at school, then this?

Anyway, I just got back from the party and had to tell someone. I realize that you're not exactly someone anymore ... but you are to me.

Sticks

March 8th

Dear Stones,

So, I'm already starting to re-think this whole track team thing. I know it's only been a few weeks since I made the team, but I had no idea how many practices we were going to have. My mom wanted me to be busy, but this is ridiculous. I feel like all I do is go to school, run, play guitar, homework, sleep, and repeat. Oh, and fit in the weekly OC appointment. Can't forget that!

I haven't had much time to do anything, including keeping you updated. I've been so busy that some days I even forget to think about you. It's not that I forget—it's just that the whole day can go by and, before I know it, I'm in bed and too tired to think. It used to be that moment after going to bed but right before falling asleep that I'd think about you the most. But lately I've been too tired and, as soon as my head hits the pillow, I'm out. Is this what they all want? Me to be so busy that I can't think about you? Is this what's going to happen? I gradually stop thinking about you until I don't think about you at all. Is that what it means to move on with my life?

Does moving on with my life mean forgetting yours?

I promise that won't happen. No matter how much they get me to do, how busy they keep me, I won't forget you.

Sticks

*March 11*th

Dear Kacey,

Did you do this because I said I was starting to move on?
Did you?

Things were finally starting to feel—not normal, because
I don't think things will ever feel normal again, but
better. I'm on the track team. Which doesn't make me an
"athlete," but it does mean that I can sit with some of them
at lunch now. People still look at me different in the halls
sometimes, but there are fewer of them—in general, things
were getting better. I was dealing. I was moving on ... I was
trying to move on and then ... the note.

And it can't just be a coincidence. It had to be you.

A note.

Your note.

Your suicide note.

To me.

It's sitting beside me right now. You used that Calvin and Hobbes stationery I gave you, like, six Christmases ago. Why did you use that?

My mom said that your mom called and asked to see me. At Christmas, I told your mom that I'd come by to visit more. I meant it when I said it. I planned on coming by to see your parents and your brother so many times. I even walked over a few times, but I just couldn't do it. It's just not the same without you there. Obviously.

When my mom first told me that your mom had something "very important" to tell me, I thought maybe she was just saying that to get me over to your house. All the way over, I was hoping it was just that and nothing serious, but I knew even before I got there, it was something ...

When your mom answered the door, she gave me a big hug. She seemed to be in really good spirits. I didn't see your dad while I was there, but Owen ran down the stairs and tackled me as soon as I came in. He held me so tight ... I feel really bad for not going to visit him. First you leave and then me. Anyway, I followed your mom up to your room. I felt like I was going to lose it, like that day with the frog.

I was shaking, dizzy. I thought I was going to throw up on the hardwood floor. Then Owen grabbed my hand and smiled. I smiled back. He pulled me down the hall and we went into your room.

Kacey, your room is exactly as you left it. It was trippy. I kept waiting for you to walk out of your bathroom or something. Your mom said that she couldn't go in your room for months, and, when she finally did, she didn't want to touch anything. I guess something changed. Maybe she's trying to move on, too, because she finally decided to make your bed or wash the sheets ... I'm not sure which one. She told me but I can't remember. Anyway, that's when she found them ... notes. Three of them under your pillow.

One to your parents.

One for Owen.

And one for me.

She gave me the note, and she also gave me that picture of us when we were twelve and I went camping with your family that summer.

It's the picture where we're wading in the river, looking for crayfish. We're both holding one up in the air and waving. I remember that right after that picture was taken, we made the crayfish fight each other. Mine won. That was an epic summer. That's where "Sticks and Stones" got started. The picture frame still has some of those sticks and stones we found, glued to the outside. Mostly it's just globs of dried glue spots where things used to be, but some stuff hung on.

You'd always called me "Sticks," ever since we were little. Then we met those boys that summer, the ones who camped across the river and tried to take our swimming hole. They heard you call me Sticks, and they started making fun of us, chanting something about sticks and stones. I wanted to leave, but you just threatened to throw a big rock at them and yelled, "That's right. Now get out of here or you'll really find out that sticks and stones CAN break your bones." OMG, I've never seen boys run so fast. They stayed away from us the rest of the week ... that was awesome.

I can't open it.

Not right now.

Forever, Sticks

March 12th

Stones,

You left me a note, and then your little brother blabbed about the note to his friends, and then they blabbed about the note to their older siblings, and then they blabbed about the note to everyone else, and now everyone in the world knows that you left me a note.

So much for things being semi-normal. So much for "moving on."

Why couldn't you just let me move on?

It took a really long time but, finally, after all these months, people weren't staring at me when I walked down the hall or tried to eat my lunch. That's how I knew something was up today when I came to school. I got my books out of my locker and walked to first block, and I could feel everyone staring at me and doing that whisper thing as I walked by.

I didn't know what was going on until Drea cornered me before English. She had to know if the rumors were true and if you had left *me* a note. *Me* ... like, how could you leave a note to *me* and not her? She didn't say that, but I know that's what she was thinking.

We had a fight. I called her a bitch, and then I said that of course you left *me* a note, because as much as she wants to pretend that you two were best friends, everyone knows that you were my best friend, and she is just using your death to get popular. And then I said ... I feel so bad about this ... but then I said that you didn't even like her, and that you only hung out with her because you felt sorry for her when she first came to school and didn't know anyone else.

I know I went too far. And I know I shouldn't have said it. I don't know why I did. Drea ran off crying, and now everyone knows that you really did leave me a note. This just happened, by the way. Like, ten minutes ago. I'm sitting in that little room beside English class that they use for test writing and trouble students, because Miss Baker heard the whole thing and her supervisor was there, too. Her supervisor is this really old lady, who smells like tea and spearmint gum and sometimes sits at the back of the class and writes notes about Baker's teaching, while she annoyingly clears her throat every two minutes. Anyway, Baker got really mad that we caused a scene in her class, so she put me in this room for the rest of the block. I feel kind of bad that I got her in trouble. It's Drea's fault.

So, you won't believe this, but Jake just came to see me. He said that Baker sent him to give me today's work, and to tell me that she wants to see me after class. As he was leaving, he stopped and asked me ...

Jake: You don't have to tell me if you don't want to. But, is it true? About the note thing?

I wouldn't have told him but it was the way he was asking. He wasn't prying to know the latest gossip like everyone else. He was just ... genuinely asking.

Me: Yes.
Jake: Whoa. Did you ...
Me: Not yet. I can't.
Jake: Ya, that's some pretty heavy stuff.
Me: (I didn't say anything. I just nodded.)
Jake: I wish I had gotten to know her better. We sat next to each other in science sometimes. She seemed pretty cool.
Me: She was.
Jake: And, hey, don't let Drea get to you. She can be a bitch sometimes.
Me: I know.
Jake: So, uh ... Baker has just assigned this final project for *Romeo and Juliet*. Do you want to be partners?
Me: With you?
Jake: If you want.
Me: Yeah, sure, okay. What is it?
Jake: Cool. (And then he smiled like I just agreed to go out on a date or something.) The project topics are in the

sheets I just gave you. I'll let you pick the topic. I better get back to class.

Me: Okay. I guess we'll talk later.

Jake: Later.

I don't get him. He's cute, athletic, and he could be the most popular guy in school, but it's almost like he's above it all. Not in a snobby way, just in a "this place is really lame and I got other things to do" type of way. And he's always so quiet. It's like he's taking everything in, always thinking about stuff. Maybe's he's trying to be that cool, mysterious guy. Or maybe that's actually him. And no, I don't have a crush if that's what you're thinking. I'm just ... curious about him, that's all.

Well, I better get some work done so Baker doesn't totally lose it on me later.

Sticks

It's only been a few hours since I wrote you last, but soooo much has happened since. After the bell, I went back to class to apologize to Baker. Her supervisor was still there, and Baker must have told her something about me, because when I walked in, she was leaving and she hugged me when she walked by. Awkward, much!! I apologized to Baker. She was pretty understanding about it all, but I could tell that she was a little angry, which was kind of refreshing. She asked what the argument was about. I told her about your note. I feel like she's the only person in the entire school, maybe the city, who didn't know. She didn't ask, but I told her that I hadn't read it yet. She said I'll read it when I'm ready. I'll have to be considering it's some of the "last words you ever wrote." Something she said, not me.

Your "*last words*" ... I hadn't really thought about it that way. Leave it to an English teacher to make it more serious than it has to be. Oh, and Baker asked me what topic I'd like to focus on for the final *Romeo and Juliet* project. I told her that I wanted to focus on the ending ... on the suicides. At first she didn't think it was a good idea, but I told her that I feel like it's something I need to do. And I do. I also think it's a topic I know well now. She told me to think about it over the weekend and, if I still wanted to do it on Monday, I could. But I don't need to think about it. I want to do this. I hope Jake will be okay with it. I'm pretty sure my mom would throw a spaz if she knew about it. I'm not going to tell her.

Anyway, there's something else ... something BIG. After I left school, my mom texted to say that we had something to talk about when she got home. I was sure that it was about Drea, but it was actually about you ... well, your parents. They've decided to get a divorce. I know that you're not surprised. I guess your parents are going to share custody of Owen. My mom said that your mom said it was because of something you wrote in your letter to them. I'm not worried about your parents. We both know this is better for them and I guess, in a way, this is better for Owen—but this, after you ... I'm going over to see him.

Sticks

*March 13*th

Stones,

Your parents finally filed for a divorce. I'm guessing you knew this would happen, since you practically gave them the green light in your letter to them. I don't actually know what you said in your letter, but your mom mentioned a few things. She seemed in a much better mood. One of the best moods I've seen her in in a really long time. I know that you told her that it wasn't her fault, and that you hoped they would finally get a divorce and just be happier. That it was okay for them to be happy. Whatever else you said, I think she needed to hear. I mean, she's not totally back to her old self, but she's better than I thought she'd be. She was grateful that I came over to check in on Owen. He's ... not doing as well as she is.

I found him in his closet, playing games on the iPad.

He was happy to see me. We hung out for a bit and he showed me your letter. I didn't want to read it, but he was really excited for me to see it—like it was show and tell or something. I just skimmed it. I still don't think he gets what happened to you, just that you're gone. And like you said in the letter, when he gets older he might understand and be able to forgive you. Although, I don't ... understand, I mean. And I'm not sure I forgive you, either.

He really wanted me to show him the one you left for me. He didn't get that I hadn't read it yet. No one gets it. My mom says she understands, but she keeps "checking in" with me. And even though she doesn't ask, I know it's to see if I opened it yet. Anyway, Owen got really mad at me and threw a mini-tantrum. I felt bad, but your mom told me not to worry and that it was probably better if I left. So I did. It's going to take some time, but I think the little booger will be okay ... eventually.

Sticks

*March 18*th

Dear Kacey,

You chose to leave. Do you know how many people don't get the choice? There are cancers and accidents that don't give people a choice between life and death, but you—you chose to die. Suicide. No one wants to hear or say this word. It's, like, taboo or something. It freaks people out. Like the school. They've totally avoided talking about what you actually did. I think I scare the admin because I know what you did and I was closest to you. My mom is freaked out by it—it's like they all think it's contagious and, since I was closest to you, maybe I have it in me, too. I think if I had it in me, I'd know ... but then again, I couldn't spot it in you.

I'm doing all this research about it for the R&J project. Did you know that suicide is one of the leading causes of death in teens? Number three, actually, after accidents and cancer. Knowing you, you already knew that. You probably looked into it before you did it. And all the Internet sites say that the act of actually killing oneself is so contrary to human nature and our instinct to survive that it indicates a mental illness. So, maybe you WERE sick. Maybe this was your character flaw.

I'm just finding out so much right now. Apparently, while more girls attempt suicide, more guys are successful because they choose ways that are more violent and final. Shakespeare should have done his research, because he got it wrong. Juliet should have drunk the poison and Romeo should have stabbed himself. That would have been more realistic.

Jake agrees with me. I've kind of taken over the project. It's not that he doesn't want to help, but I've become a bit obsessed and I think it's freaking him out. I can tell he's worried that I'm taking this suicide project a little too far. He's supportive, though. And he doesn't think it's right that the school just ignored the whole thing. He said that he'd help me get some petitions signed if I wanted to protest or something. I know he was joking, but it got me thinking that maybe I should be doing something more for you. And not just for you but for others, too. I don't know ... my mom would probably freak all over again. I'd probably have to go to more OC appointments ... people would get all worried about me again ... maybe it is best to just leave it.

Sticks

March 20th

Dear Stones,

So, I've become a track star. Really. We had a track meet today. I didn't want to go. I was in no mood to do anything, and I told my mom I'd rather be working on my project for school, but she gave me some crap about making a commitment and how I really need to be there for my teammates ... which erupted into a huge fight about you. I don't even know how we got there. I ended up going just to get away from her.

The coach put me in the 3000-meter event. I guess I had some pent-up anger or energy, or something was going on, because I won by almost a half lap over the next girl. Jake and I ended up hanging out after. I forgot to tell you, but he asked me a few days ago, while we were working on the project, if I wanted to do something after the track meet. He won, too.

We got an iced-frap and went for a walk near the park. He's actually a lot cooler than I thought, and smarter, too. The only reason he's always sleeping in class is because he gets up for practice at, like, 4 AM. His parents want him to become the next Crosby, but he just likes to play because his mom likes to watch him. He said his mom has Multiple Sclerosis and she's in a wheelchair. I felt bad because I didn't even know what that was until I looked it up on the Internet. He has two younger sisters and I think he has to help out at home a lot. He's not at all the guy I thought he was. We got into this really deep conversation about you. He's all quiet at school but he sees everything. He knew you and I hadn't been the same this past year ... before you committed suicide. I don't know how, but I feel like he gets me ... gets what I've been going through. What I've really been going through.

Jake: What was Kacey like?

I didn't say anything at first. And I think he felt me tense up because then he said...

Jake: I'm sorry. We don't have to talk about her if you don't want to.

Me: No. It's okay ... She was ... I don't know ... smart. Like, really smart. She used to piss off all the teachers and adults because she liked to challenge them, just to see if she could get a rise out of them.

Jake: (laughing) Really?

Me: Yeah. And... ever since I knew her, she loved to read, but she didn't like it when other people knew that about her. It was like reading was just for her and she wanted to keep it that way. Not because she felt it would wreck her image or anything—she didn't care about stuff like that ... I admired her for that. And talented, although she'd hate it if she heard me say that. She could hear a song a few times and then be able to mimic it on the guitar. Sometimes she even made the songs better. But she hated messing up. Like, really hated it. She didn't like making mistakes or being wrong.

Jake: I get that. My hockey coach says I can be my own worst enemy.

Me: Kacey was like that, too. Sometimes she would get so down on herself because of it. When she was like that, it was hard to talk to her. She had all this energy and, when she was happy, she was really happy. And it was contagious; everyone around her would be happy, too. That's what I loved about her the most. Sometimes she didn't have to say or do anything to make me smile. But then ... if she was mad, or upset, she was like another person. She could say the meanest things. She'd always feel bad about it later. And no matter what she said or did, I'd always forgive her because she was my Stones, and she could play a song, make me laugh, make me forget about how mad I was at her.

Jake: Stones?

Me: That's what I called her. And she called me Sticks.

Jake: Sticks and Stones?

Me: There's a whole story to it. It was our thing.

And then I got sad and quiet, but Jake didn't say anything or make me think I had to talk. He just sat there with me, waiting.

Me: She was so creative. She had so much energy when she was excited about something, like some amazing song lyric she wrote. Sometimes she would phone me in the middle of the night just to tell me about it. She could be ... I don't want to say "consuming," because that might sound bad ... but sometimes she could be like that. She was ... she was ... I don't know ... Kacey. She was my best friend. And I miss her.

Jake: That's a lot to miss.

Me: She is.

After we talked, he walked me home and that was it. We didn't kiss or anything like that. I'm not sure I like him that way. It was just nice to talk with him. I think he felt the same way. Anyway, I promised him that I'd finish up this project for Monday. He thinks we've done enough. I don't know if I'll ever think that.

Sticks

March 22nd

Stones,

I still don't get why you left.

I've been reading all this stuff about depression and signs of suicide, and okay, like, you showed some signs, but so does everyone else I know. Were you depressed? All the adults and doctors say you were. I'm not convinced, but you must have been. Did you ever talk about death or stuff like that? Well, you wrote some pretty dark poems and songs. And I guess we talked about who would come to our funerals if we died, and how we never wanted to die in a fire or something. Did you start those conversations?

Maybe I should have watched you more or been closer. I know that's what everyone wonders about me. How could I have not seen it? Why didn't I see it?

I don't know. Maybe I did, but I never thought you were

capable of it. You never outright said you were thinking about killing yourself. Even if you had, I'm not sure I would have taken you seriously.

It doesn't make any sense. We weren't as close as we used to be but we were still friends, and you made plans to hang out with me that weekend. We were supposed to go to a movie. I read on the Internet that people who are planning to commit suicide usually don't make future plans. But we had lots. You had lots. At least, I thought you did ... but you didn't really. Not real plans.

I keep thinking about that day. Did you think about it all day? Did you know all day long that you were going to do that after the party? When I saw you, you didn't seem any different. I just keep wondering if I'd done something different that day ... if I went home with you that night ... if I had told you to stay ... the obnoxious counselor keeps telling me that wouldn't have made a difference, but how the fuck does she know??

Sticks

March 24ᵗʰ

Dear Stones,

So, it finally happened. The thing that everyone was waiting for ...

I had a meltdown in class. And it was pretty epic.

I don't know why I lost it. I got up in a pretty good mood. I finished the project early and felt like it was ready to present. But then when I went down for breakfast, my mom was getting mad at Hershey for peeing on the floor. I didn't like her yelling at Hershey so, of course we had a big fight. I said some things and she started crying. I've been making her cry a lot lately. I was going to say sorry, but then my dad got mad at me, too, and I just stormed out. So there was that.

Then, I was spending part of first block in the bathroom, going through my phone, looking at photos of you—MY PHONE!!—I'll get to that part. It was just coincidence, but my bathroom buddy was there. I was telling her about the fight with my mom when these girls walked in. They were "like, totally" chatty and talking about their weekend. One of them said something about being asked to go to this party or something, and she said, "Ya, right, like I'd go there. I'd rather kill myself." Normally I would have stayed hidden, but today I couldn't. I walked out and all of them stopped talking and looked at me. You should have seen the look on their faces. I didn't say anything. I didn't have to. They all left really quickly—and then my bathroom buddy came out—Loren's younger sister Mia!! I don't know why I got so angry—cuz I finally saw my mysterious bathroom buddy, and it is someone I should have known all along, or because she is only in Grade 9 (which makes me feel totally stupid), or because she is Loren's sister? I yelled at her for that. The first thing I did was accuse her of telling Loren everything we talked about. She denied it and said that Loren didn't know she was talking to me. I told her to get out and she ran away. She actually looked scared of me.

And then I had to do that presentation in English. And I guess everything just kind of erupted at once—the perfect storm. Jake knew there was something wrong before we even started, but when he asked me what was up, I told him it was none of his business. I'm such a bitch. He started the presentation by giving all these facts about teen suicide, but then something in me snapped. I interrupted him and took over. I just went into a rant ...

Me: If you want to know the truth, Romeo and Juliet were stupid teenagers, who were selfish and didn't think about the consequences of their actions, or who they were leaving behind. Shakespeare's an idiot. Romeo and Juliet didn't kill themselves for love. They can say it was for love, but they're still dead, and now they have no one to love and no one wins. We shouldn't feel sorry for them—they COMMITTED SUICIDE. They KILLED themselves. It's not romantic; it's not heroic; it's not even tragic ... it's just a fucking waste. Why don't we say what it is they actually did?

They chose to stop living.

And then it became about you. Or maybe it was always about you.

I knew I was losing it in front of everyone, including Jake, who was watching me from the side, looking at me like I was a crazy person. But I couldn't stop myself. We all pretend like you're just gone, but the truth is you died, you killed yourself, and no one wants to say it out loud.

Someone must have told the principal that I was having a meltdown in English, because he walked in ... and seeing his face just set me off more.

Me: (yelling) We need to acknowledge what Romeo and Juliet and Kacey did. SUICIDE. And the school can't hide from it because the truth is we're all to blame for her death. And that's where Shakespeare got it right. Their parents, their friends, the nurse, that stupid friar, Mercutio, Tybalt ... they all saw it coming. They just didn't want to believe it could actually happen until it was too late to do anything.

breaking into pieces. And we can try to glue it together, but we know there's always going to be fine lines of cracks showing and a piece missing. Our friendship will never be what it was. We lost you and, because of that, we lost each other. Since you died, we've changed, as a group and as individuals—I don't know if it's a good or bad thing. It's just the way it is.

I finally went home after a few hours with the girls. I told them what happened to my phone, and they said they would send me some of the pictures and videos that they have of you. It won't be the same but it's nice of them. We know that we're going to see each other at school, but we still said our goodbyes. When I got home, my mom was sitting on the couch, petting Hershey and crying. I was prepared for her to get mad and yell at me, but I wasn't prepared to see her like that. I told her I was sorry, but she just got up off the couch and held me. And I started crying again. I think I've cried more today than I've cried my whole life. Seriously.

My mom thinks I've been holding it all in since your funeral, and maybe she's right. We didn't really talk at all. She just cuddled me on the couch the way she used to when I was a kid. Miss Baker phoned and told her what happened. I guess she feels totally responsible for letting me do the assignment. My mom said that Baker is so upset about what happened that she might not finish her practicum. There's a big meeting I have to go to tomorrow. The oc, Baker, Principal Kline, my parents—they'll all be there. I don't know what's going to happen. I'm too tired to think about it right now, anyway.

Night.

Sticks

Oh ... and I messaged Jake on FB to apologize about freaking out and wrecking our presentation. He just messaged back.

> Are you kidding? That was the best prezzie EVER! I hope you're ok =)

So I guess we're good. I hope we are.

*April 7*th

Dear Stones,

The counselor said I can stop writing to you if I want. She's not going to check it anymore, and I only have to go and see her if I want to. But I have a few pages of this journal left and, besides, you should know what happened.

When my parents and I walked into Kline's office, everyone was there waiting for us. I thought this was going to be another meeting where everyone talked about what they were going to do with me, but that's not what happened at all. I don't know how it happened, but I guess Baker showed our final project report on *Romeo and Juliet* to Kline. Then they spoke to my counselor and got her take on me and on everything that had been going on. Anyway, the principal agreed with what I said and what I wrote.

Kline: Sara, what you said about Kacey and the school not doing enough ... well, we discussed it further and we agree. Perhaps we did not handle the situation ...

Me: Stop saying that about her. She is not a situation.

Kline: You're right. I apologize. What I am trying to say is that we should have done more. We are going to do more.

Me: How?

Kline: How would you feel about going around with Julie (the obnoxious counselor does have a name) and speaking with a few classes about Kacey, about the topic of suicide ...

Mom: I'm not sure that's *such* a good idea ...

Me: Mom, it's okay.

Mom: Sara, I ...

Me: No, Mom, really. It's okay.

Mom: If you're sure.

Me: I am. It's just ... I wouldn't know what to say.

Baker: I think you just need to be honest. Talk about you and what you went through after Kacey left.

Julie: And I'll be with you the whole time.

Kline: What do you think, Sara?

I'd told them I'd think about it. Me!? Some teen-suicide-prevention spokesperson? I feel like this is something I need to talk to you about, like I need your thoughts. I'd be talking about you and I'm not sure you'd be okay with that. I know you wouldn't be. But then again ... you're not here. When you killed yourself, you kind of lost the right to have an opinion. I think I've already made up my mind. I just thought you should know ... and I do hope you understand.

Sticks

Oh, and my parents got me a new phone to replace the one I dropped in the ocean. It's a way better one. It must have cost them a fortune, but they said my birthday is coming up. I know they just feel bad about the photos and stuff I lost. I guess I should be happy about it. It's just that nothing can replace what's gone.

*April 20*th

Dear Stones,

I've been sitting here, looking at the journal for about ten minutes, thinking about what I wanted to say to you. It's been about two weeks since I wrote anything, and I felt you deserved some kind of an update.

I don't know where a person goes when they die—maybe you really can see down from wherever you are and, if you can, you probably already know everything I'm about to tell you. But just in case you can't, and this is the only way you're getting to know what's going on here (like a spirit journal or something—nothing freaky, just kind of magical), then I think you should know a few things.

Things have gone pretty much back to normal. I mean, people aren't looking at me like the girl who went ballistic in Baker's class. They're back to looking at me like the girl whose best friend killed herself. I'm not sure that will ever go away. I've gotten used to it. Baker decided to finish her practicum. It took some convincing from me and my mom. But I think she's going to make a great teacher one day, so I'm glad she didn't quit because of me. Actually, she's going to help organize some of the talks with other schools. We haven't even done the first talk with our school, but they're already planning others—well, I'm in on it, too ... and so is your mom. We'll all be going around together and talking with students about you and what we went through when you left. We have our first talk in a couple of days. It's with the whole 11th grade. We figured we'd start with the people who knew you the best. I'm super nervous about it, but Baker reminded me that I have this journal and I should just look to it if I don't know what to say. Although, based on my whole *Romeo and Juliet* project, she's sure I won't be at a loss for words!

It's funny—until she called it "my journal," I kind of thought of it as yours. In some ways, I still do.

Loren, Drea, and I haven't spoken since that day on the beach. I knew we wouldn't. But we smile and say hi in the halls and stuff. I also see Melissa (aka, Weird Glasses Girl) sometimes. Usually she's eating by herself in the library or sitting by herself on the stairs. We don't talk a lot but, when I do see her, I usually smile and, sometimes, when I see her in the library, I'll grab a book and sit next to her. I wish high school was better for her. I wish it was better for a lot of us.

But the reality is, high school is high school ... and it can really suck sometimes.

Oh, and Mia found me in the bathroom, not hiding in a stall, just washing my hands. I said I was sorry for yelling at her. She asked if we could still meet to talk about stuff sometimes, not in the bathroom, just like normal, in the lunchroom or somewhere. All this time, I thought she was meeting me so I could do the talking, but I think she needed me just as much as I needed her. I thought about your poem, and those *uncontrollable ripples* you wrote about. A stone dropping in the water causes a ripple effect, and you can't control or imagine just how far those ripples will go. Mia only knew you through Loren. She didn't really know you, but your death affected her sister and, to some degree, her as well. She's struggling to understand why just as much as we all are.

And yesterday I raced in the city championship for track. I came third, but the coach was really happy because our team won the overall. I might run again next year. I might not. We'll see. I do love running, though. I take Hershey for a run all the time now.

Jake won his events so we went out to celebrate. I think we might be dating but I don't know. We haven't made anything official. I went to watch him play hockey. He let me play bad guitar for him. We haven't kissed or anything... but I want to. See, this is the kind of thing that I wish you were here to talk about with. I still miss you. Sometimes I miss you so much, it actually literally hurts, like a real pain in my chest—maybe it's my heart. Can a sixteen-year-old have a heart attack?

So that's what's going on with me.

Sticks

May 1st

Dear Kacey,

We had our big assembly today. We did it in the gym. Our whole class was there. They dimmed the lights and had a big screen up at the front. Julie gave a PowerPoint presentation about suicide. It was a really good presentation ... she's not so obnoxious after all. Actually, she's kind of cool, but I'm never going to tell her that.

We put your picture up on the screen. Don't worry, it wasn't a lame school picture. It was that one of you from our last sleepover. You were wearing your purple hoodie and you're kind of laughing at something ... it's a good pic, and it's so you. I couldn't look at it when we put it up. I almost lost it before I even started talking. Drea and Loren both saw that I was struggling, so they came down and sat beside me. It was hard to get started but, once I did, I just talked about you and all the stuff I've been dealing with since you left.

A lot of students had questions about it. I don't know who asked it, but someone in the back asked if we know why you did it. I think they, like me and everyone else, need a reason. Your mom got up to answer. It wasn't easy for her to talk, but she said that it's important everyone understands that you're the only one who can fully answer that question. The doctors can put a label on it but, in the end, you had your own reasons. And we may never fully understand why you did what you did, but we do have to live with it. I have to live with it. Your mom was actually pretty great.

There was only one question I had a hard time answering. Nikki Harris wanted to know how I found out and what I went through that day. I didn't know what to say, so I brought out this journal and I read about that day. It was the February 17th entry. At the end, I read that I didn't know why I had written about that day. Something about not knowing the point of it at the time ... but I understand now, not completely, but sort of.

I'm on the last page of this journal and I'm running out of room. I guess this is it.

I'm totally going to miss you.

Kacey, I'm sorry I wasn't there for you when you needed me to be. I'm sorry we had started drifting apart. I'm sorry I never told you to stay at the party. I'm sorry I never texted you back. I'm sorry that you felt you had to leave. I'm sorry that we won't get to grow old together and that the world will never hear your music. I'm sorry.

I don't mind if you come to visit me. I hope that I'll always be able to see, hear, and feel you around me. You left, but I hope that you're never gone.

Forever, your Sticks.

Sara

Sticks,

I know I'm not in any place to ask you a favor, but I'm going to anyway. When I'm gone, I want you to remember me for me and not what I did or how I died. I don't want my life, or yours, to be about my death. I don't want you to think about me in that way. When you think about me, I want you to think about banana-chocolate milkshakes, skipping school to go for one of our epic chats by the ocean, sleepovers, scary movie nights, camping, marshmallow fights, my cheesy campfire music ... and please don't make me out to be some saint, either. We both know I wasn't that. I know I haven't been the easiest friend to be around this year, but thanks for "sticking" by me. I might have been your Stones but you were my rock, and you're so much stronger than you know. You're not going to get it, and I don't want you to. I know there's nothing I can write that is going to make this any easier on you. Please don't hate me for this.

Love me for who I was.

Forever, your Stones.

Kacey

Acknowledgments

Bree—thank you for reading and rereading and then reading again. Thank you for handling my ego with care. Thank you for your honesty and vulnerability. Thank you for sharing Trevor with me.

Peter—thank you for believing in the importance of this story and for giving *Kacey* a home with Red Deer. Thank you for your guidance. Thank you for putting me into uncomfortable places and helping me to take this story and myself somewhere I didn't know we could go.

Jen—thank you for your friendship; I think you will spot pieces of it throughout this story. Thank you for listening to me all these years.

Kimmy—thank you for always asking me to tell you a story.

All my family and friends—I am blessed to have you in my life. Thank you for your encouragement and patience.

Grandma and Grandpa—thank you for telling me that I could do anything, and, more importantly, for making me believe it. I miss you both.

Mom—thank you. Forever—love you.

Suicide Information and Resources

The way through it ...

Reading Kacey's journal may bring up all kinds of feelings, whether you have been depressed yourself, thought about hurting yourself, or are worried about someone else. That's okay, because when we feel things, it lets us know there might be something we need to do to take care of ourselves.

The first thing to know is that your feelings are real and are okay. Even if you don't know exactly what's going on and can't put words to your feelings, you should talk to someone you trust. If you have no one you feel comfortable talking to right now, then it's important to call a crisis line like KidsHelpPhone or a local distress center (numbers are listed below).

There is a way through it.

That's what you need to remember in your lowest moments. So hold on, there is a listening ear, even if you don't know that yet.

As Good Charlotte wrote in their suicide prevention song:
Hold on, if you feel like letting go
Hold on, it gets better than you know.
Don't stop looking, you're one step closer.
Don't stop searching, it's not over.
Hold on.
(*Hold On* by Good Charlotte, 2002)

The facts

People talk about these being the best years of your life, but the facts are that young people struggle. There's so much going on between the ages of 12 and 25. Our bodies go through their biggest growth period at this time. Our brains are changing constantly, making us unsure of how to react or what choices to make. Our social and intellectual development—making new friends, finding new interests, questioning what we thought was true—make this time even more challenging.

And then there is the stress. People think that young adults don't have much stress but that's not true. The pressure of school, starting a new job, expectations of family and community, and feeling unsure of our abilities, can sometimes make life feel overwhelming. You are not alone in your struggle. All young adults face these challenges.

Some of us find stress hard to handle and need help to deal with it. In fact young adults are more stressed out than any other age group.

More than one in five young adults struggle with their mental health, most often anxiety and depression. When we are depressed we feel isolated, lose hope, and sometimes harm ourselves. Feeling anxious is normal. It helps us to avoid danger. But when it gets in the way of our leading the life we want—when we have extreme physical and emotional responses to things—then it is no longer a useful feeling.

Suicide is the second leading cause of death for young people. Canada has the fourth highest rate of suicide for young adults in the 34 countries of The Organisation for Economic Co-operation and Development (OECD). And if you are poor, if you have experienced some sort of trauma like abuse or bullying, or if you identify as different from the majority of your peers, then you are at greater danger of experiencing mental health issues.

How to help
Research shows that talking openly to people about suicide in a safe and supportive environment does not increase your risk of committing suicide but instead lessens it. Most people contemplating suicide need to feel hope that the emotional pain they are experiencing will lessen. One of the best ways to give them hope is to offer them some

alternatives and show them we care. Whether you are a friend, a teacher or a parent, these discussions are hard to have. Therefore it's important to look for support and resources in your community.

If you know someone who's struggling, the first thing to do is to listen. This doesn't mean you have to have all the answers. You can always say you get it but you don't know the answer and will help the person find out. Find someone to help you get some answers—like your parents, your friends, another family member, your guidance counselor, or a teacher you trust. There is a lot of information out there and people are more open to discussing mental health than ever before.

One way to detect an emerging problem is to look for behavior in your friend or child or student that doesn't make sense: an unlikely change, looking bad, being crabby or twitchy, complaining about not sleeping, drinking more, doing more drugs, eating differently, pulling away from friends, doing wild and risky things more than usual, or giving things away (when they don't usually do that)—or just plain acting differently.

Learning about mental health is essential. Just as we must learn how to take care of our bodies, so must we learn how to take of our hearts and minds. There are tons of resources online (some are listed below) and a trusted doctor or guidance counselor will also have great information. Or you could join a support group at school or in your community. Many school boards are committed to integrating education about mental health into their curriculum and teacher training (see for instance the Toronto District School Board site). This is also true of universities, many of which have growing support networks on their campuses (see the Jack Project and on-campus peer supports that often are available through student services).

If the burden of your friend's pain becomes too heavy for you to carry, you must get help for yourself and for her or him. If your friend or child or student has said "I don't think it's worth living anymore" or "Nobody cares if I'm alive or dead," take it seriously. This is a cry for help ... yes, they are seeking attention but they are seeking it because they are in terrible pain. Even if your friend has sworn you to secrecy, it's okay to break a promise to save a life.

Sometimes when a young person close to you hurts herself you feel you could have done something to prevent it. It's normal to feel that way but the thing is, you are not responsible! Sometimes the pain is too great for any of us to take it away.

If you lose someone to suicide or feel depressed yourself, remember Kacey and Sara's story. You may not feel exactly as they did but whatever your feelings, they are important and real.

There is a way through and a way to move on.

Resources

In every province, there is a Mental Health Crisis Line, hotline, health line, distress line, help line, or a suicide line that you can find online. In most provinces, you can call **2-1-1** for information about other mental health services.

(This is true of every province except Manitoba and Newfoundland, and it is coming soon to Nunavut but is not available in the Northwest Territories or the Yukon.)

In the United States, the National Suicide Prevention Lifeline (www.suicidepreventionlifeline.org) provides help line phone services and other resources regionally across the country. As well, its You Matter branch (www.youmatter. suicidepreventionlifeline.org) offers helpful information, resources as well as a blog specifically for young adults.

Websites with resources and more information:
Kidshelp phone (ages 5 to 20):
http://www.kidshelpphone.ca/Teens/Home.aspx

Canadian suicide prevention: http://suicideprevention. ca/thinking-about-suicide/find-a-crisis-centre/ (1-800-273-8255)

Mind your mind: http://www.mindyourmind.ca/ National (USA) Suicide Prevention Lifeline (www. suicidepreventionlifeline.org) and its section for young adults, You Matter (www.youmatter.suicide preventionlifeline.org).

Mobilizing Minds project: www.mobilizingminds.ca

About Depression: www.depression.informedchoices. ca/#sthash.KHSq0GLp.dpuf

For a program in your school, talk to a guidance counsellor

The Jack Project: http://www.thejackproject.org/

For LGBT youth: www.itgetsbetter.org and **The Trevor**

Project: www.thetrevorproject.org

Providing mental health resources to young people:
The Kelty Patrick Dennehy Foundation www.
thekeltyfoundation.org

To learn more about mental health:
Canadian Mental Health Association: http://www.cmha.
ca/mental-health/your-mental-health/youth/
   The Mental Health Commission of Canada: http://
www.mentalhealthcommission.ca/English/issues/child-
and-youth

For adults wanting to take a mental health first aid course
go to: http://www.mentalhealthfirstaid.ca/EN/course/
descriptions/Pages/MHFAforYouth.aspx

Contributed by **Jenny Carver**, Executive Director, Stella's
Place www.stellasplace.ca. Stella's Place is a street front
and online community being developed by parents, young
adults, and experts to respond to the mental health needs
of young adults in the Toronto area. It will engage with
people between 15 and 29 with a full range of clinical and
alternative ways to help them find their way through to
recovery and connection. Stella's Place will be open in the
fall of 2015.

Photo credit: Sarah Baas

Interview with Dawn Green

What led you to write this story?

To be honest, I had the title first. I was in a local bookstore and I had a vision (I guess you could call it) of a book (my book) on the shelf called *When Kacey Left*. I knew it was going to be about a girl dealing with the loss of a friend but I wasn't sure in what capacity. I logged it in the back of my mind and it wasn't until a couple of years later, sitting in an education course at university discussing the topic teen suicide, that "Kacey" spoke to me.

For me, this story was always going to focus on those left behind, dealing with this empty space in their life. Suicide can be such a taboo topic. And losing someone to suicide is difficult / sad / frustrating because those left behind are left with so many unanswered questions.

To make a long answer even longer, I met Bree, a fellow student in my education cohort and for some reason—I barely knew her at this point—I asked if she would be interested in editing this novel I was working on. I didn't know it at the time but she had always thought about pursuing editing as a profession and she divulged to me that this story was particularly important to her, as she had been directly affected by a friend's suicide. So, many things came together and *Kacey* became a story I felt I had to write.

In telling the story, though it is all told from Sara's viewpoint, you have also included other voices—parents, school authorities, other friends. Why did you think each of these voices was important for us to hear?

This story was always going to be about a friend dealing with the loss of a friend and I chose Sara—someone who felt she knew her the best—to tell it, but I also included the voices of those around her because I wanted to explore the far reaching impact of Kacey's death in Sara's world. The old adage that everyone deals with death in her or his own way is very true, but it can be difficult to understand for a teenager who is dealing with death for the first time and who has her own ideas of how people should be responding. I also wanted the other characters to reveal more about Sara—as she is reflected in their eyes. It's through the other people in her life that Sara starts to see and understand herself a little better.

You have deliberately left the reasons for Kacey's taking her own life ambiguous. Recently a number of widely publicized events of this kind have been traced to instances of bullying. Why did you decide not to make this part of Kacey's story?

Bullying is an important issue that always needs to be talked about and addressed. As a teacher—and a human being—I am happy that it has become such an important discussion topic in schools and society and I hope it continues.

When suicides happen people generally ask the question—WHY? And they want an answer that will help them understand. Unfortunately, we can't always get that answer that we want—an answer that gives us some sense of closure. I personally wanted to address the topic of mental health and depression in teens because it is another area that I think needs more attention from schools and society. The teenage world is complicated, and teenagers are complicated. Too many times I think adults can overlook the problems that teens are facing, thinking it's just typical teenage "angst," not realizing that some of them might be dealing with anxiety issues, withdrawal, depression, and / or mental health disorders. Depression in teenagers is a very real issue and needs as much attention as bullying does.

The whole story is a series of entries in a journal by Kacey's best friend, Sara. Can you tell me about the

challenge you faced in catching the voice of a 16-year-old girl in that format?

Oh, man! In some ways it was easier to capture the voice of Sara in journal format and that is why I chose to do it this way. There is an honesty and vulnerability that comes from journal writing that I wanted Sara to have so we could experience her emotions in a raw state. The difficulty came with writing an entire novel in this fashion. I wanted to maintain that this was Sara's journal but also write a complete story, get to know Kacey, and show the voices of those around her. I hope that using dialogue, memories, text conversations etc. accomplishes that while fitting with the journal format.

I teach and coach teenagers and I am around them all the time—and in some ways I feel like a teen myself sometimes—so, finding the teenage voice was, like, not that hard.

Sara not only has to deal with her own grieving over Kacey's being gone, but also with the gossip about her and Kacey that travels throughout the school. Which do you think is harder for her to overcome?

Kacey's suicide shatters Sara's world and that world includes her home, personal, and school life—every area that Kacey would have been a part of. And in each area her death is felt a little bit differently. Again, suicide comes with an element of mystery. People want answers and they will look for those answers in the people closest to the person who has died. Kacey was Sara's best friend, everyone in the school associates Kacey with Sara and Sara with Kacey, and Sara can't escape that. Yes, she is grieving, but the gossip in the school is a part of what she has to deal with, and so are the concerns of her parents and the relationships with her friends—I don't think one is more difficult to overcome than the other.

In your experience as a teacher, how do schools generally deal with student suicide when it happens?

In my personal experience schools handle a student's suicide as best they can. Counselors are brought in and students are talked to directly and sometimes the entire school is addressed about it. But, there is an element of "let's move past this and move on as quick as we can." Sara writes about how a student died of cancer and she can remember an assembly and the dedication of a playground but with Kacey they try to get through it quickly. This is something I have seen happen. Suicide is a delicate topic and I know that a lot of administrations wrestle with how best to handle it. With so many students and faculty in one building to manage, help and deal with, it can be an impossible task to appease everyone—and maybe there is no right way.

Do you think teen suicide is more frequent now than it was in the past?

I am not sure if it is more frequent or it's just that with an increase in population and access to so many social media outlets we are more aware of it. I do think teenagers face more pressures than ever. Every generation comes with new obstacles and the current generations face an onslaught of social media pressures. Teens who were upset and needed space used to be able to come home, disappear into their room, and slam the door shut. Now, with computers and phones, they are constantly being bombarded with emails, texts, Snapchats, Facetime ... it's endless and it's almost impossible for them to turn everything off. I'm certainly not blaming social media; I'm just saying that it's a different world. Teenagers have a lot of expectations put on them and I have personally witnessed and experienced an increase in teenage anxiety disorders and depression.

While this is your first published novel, you have several other projects completed. What advice do you have for young writers who are interested in pursuing a writing career?

First of all, I need to say that I feel like a ridiculous imposter even answering this question. I still look to other authors— and it feels weird putting myself in the "author" category— for their advice. In fact, I just did a happy dance after signing on the line that said "Author" on my first contract, and I am still getting used to the feel of it next to my name. And I hope that I get to do many more happy dances!

I think a lot of pressure comes with the title of "Writer" or "Author" and sometimes that pressure can be overwhelming and paralysing. To take the pressure away I personally have to tell myself that I am not "writing," I am just "telling a story," and that helps me. I think each person needs to find their own little mantra that helps them to keep going, keep writing, and keep navigating this world. In my limited experience there is no "right" way to pursue this career. There is only the "write" way—as in, you have to write, and write a lot ... and then write some more. Like anything worthwhile, this can be a tough career to pursue but if you believe in your story then you need to stop at nothing to make others believe in it too—and with any luck (but mostly perseverance) you'll be dancing your very own happy dance one day!